ALL-OF-A-KIND FAMILY UPTOWN

SYDNEY TAYLOR

Illustrated by Mary Stevens

TAYLOR PRODUCTIONS, LTD.
NEW YORK, NY

Printed in the United States of America
For information, address GRM Associates, Inc., 290 West End Avenue, New York, NY 10023.
Telephone 212-874-5964

ISBN 0-929093-09-7

For Jo and Steve

Hazel Emerson Hall
Great Books Great Kids
Charlotte Hobbs Library
Lovell, Maine

Roland – George – Hazel – Verna

You have to wind yourself up to find courage. It's easier to submit to whatever is. You have to shake yourself and say, 'No, this isn't what I'm going to accept.'

Hazel Emerson Hall

Food's on the Table

"This is the school block, so the house can't be on this one," Ella said.

"What number is it again?" asked Charlotte.

Ella glanced at the slip of paper in her hand. "725. It must be the next block."

Directly ahead, the children could see a tall woman coming through the school gate.

"Look!" cried Sarah. "Here comes Miss Brady. She's my history teacher. Gee, it's pretty late, almost supper time, and she's just getting out."

"I thought teachers were only supposed to work till three o'clock," Gertie said.

"Well, sometimes they have special things to do which keep them late," Ella explained.

At that moment, Miss Brady saw Sarah. "Hello, Sarah. What brings you here at this hour?"

Shyly Sarah looked at Miss Brady. Teachers look so different when you meet them outside, she thought to herself. "Hello, Miss Brady," she replied. "Our aunt and uncle just moved to the next block. They want us to see their new apartment, so they invited us for supper."

"I didn't know you had so many sisters and brothers, Sarah," Miss Brady said.

Sarah grinned. "No, only one brother — little Charlie here. But we're five sisters. This is my oldest sister, Ella. She'll be graduating from high school next year, same time as I graduate from here. Next comes Henny, then me, then Charlotte, and this is Gertie."

"Quite a family. I'm very pleased to meet all of you. Tell me, are any of you girls as good in history as Sarah?"

Sarah blushed.

"Not me!" Henny answered promptly. "That's one subject I don't like!"

"Did Sarah ever tell you what I say to my class about that? 'You don't like it because you won't like it, and you won't like it because you don't like it.' Well, now, I mustn't keep you from your supper. Good-by all." She gave Sarah a pat on the shoulder. "Keep studying," she remarked, and walked on.

"History — ugh!" Henny made a face. "Names and places and *dates* to remember. It's so boring."

"Oh, but it's not!" Sarah shot back indignantly. "Not the way Miss Brady teaches. She makes it so exciting you almost wish you lived in the olden days. Since I have her, I think I like history better than any other subject! I'm going to try for the history prize when I graduate next year."

"Atta girl, Sarah!" Ella said. "Now, let's see. 721 — 723. Here it is — 725. It's a nice-looking building."

Ella glanced at the paper again. "Third floor, apartment 4," she announced.

The children trooped after her up the stoop and into the vestibule. "Shouldn't we ring the bell first?" asked Gertie.

"The buzzer's out of order," Ella replied. "Lena said we should go right up."

"Come on, Charlie, we'll swing you up the stairs," said Henny. "Take his other hand, Sarah."

Whooping with delight, Charlie was borne up the stairs with his feet never once touching the ground.

Henny tapped on apartment door number 4.

There was no answer. She tapped again, louder, but still there was no answer.

"That's strange," Ella said. "I know Lena is expecting us." She touched the doorknob. "The door's open."

"I guess she means for us to come right in," Henny said.

"Maybe she's in the bedroom getting dressed, and she can't hear us," suggested Gertie.

"Well, let's go in and find out," Ella said, pushing open the door. "Lena! Lena, we're here!"

There was no reply.

They went through a small hall leading into a big square kitchen. "Is anybody home?" Charlotte shouted.

The house was still. The children looked around, not knowing quite what to do.

"Anyway, the food's on the table," Henny said cheerfully. Her eyes feasted on a slab of juicy homemade corned beef. "Mmm, doesn't that look good!"

"And potato salad! And cole slaw!" rejoiced Gertie. "Lena sure knows what we like."

"Look, Ella." Sarah pointed. "There's a note on the table." She picked it up and read aloud.

I had to do some more shopping. I'll be a little late. Don't wait for me. Go ahead and eat.

"Well, that's that," declared Henny. "Let's eat."

"Oh, I don't think that would be very nice," Ella said. "Let's wait a little while."

"We could finish setting the table in the meantime," suggested Sarah. "Lena must have been in an awful hurry. No plates, and just three settings of silverware."

Henny opened the door of the pantry. "Pretty dishes. Lena must have gotten a new set."

"And these kitchen chairs — they certainly are pretty, too," added Charlotte.

"Uncle Hyman must be doing well," Ella said.

In no time at all, the table was properly set. Now all that was left to do was to sit around and wait.

"I'm glad Lena has moved near to us," Gertie remarked. "Now we'll be able to see her so much more often."

"I'm hungry!" Charlie piped up. "I wanna eat!"

"We have to wait till Lena comes, Charlie," Ella told him.

"But I'm hungry now!"

"We're all hungry, Charlie," said Henny consolingly. "Couldn't you wait just a tiny bit longer?"

"Awright," Charlie said, pouting. Suddenly he spied the curtain of long, thin strands of rainbow-colored beads which hung across the doorway leading to the parlor. Off he skipped to investigate.

Grabbing a fistful, he watched gravely as the smooth beads slithered through his fingers. Before long, he was hopping in and out, giggling as the long, slippery strings fell over his face and body.

"He'll have it torn to pieces if Lena doesn't get here soon," Henny said. "Charlie!" she called out warningly. "You be careful with that curtain!"

"I wonder how long Mama will be at the Red Cross knitting club," Ella said. "I hope she gets here in time to eat with us."

"I bet she's enjoying herself," said Charlotte. "Nobody can knit like Mama — so fast and with such even stitches. No wonder all the women on the block made her join."

"We've only been at war with Germany for a month, but the Red Cross will need lots more knitters, because the boys will be called up for service any day now," added Ella.

"Will Jules go, too?" Gertie asked.

"I don't think he's old enough yet."

"Oh, where is that Lena? I'm starving!" Henny cried.

"So am I," Charlotte chimed in. "Gee, Ella, couldn't we at least get started? Lena said we should."

"I don't know. It's not very polite. What do you think, Henny?"

"She left a note, didn't she? So I say we should eat."

"There isn't too much of this stuff, so let's be careful," Ella cautioned as she spooned out the salad.

"Maybe it's because Lena's not used to cooking for a big mob like us," put in Charlotte. "There are only two of them."

"That's so, but I don't quite understand it," Ella said, as she finished slicing the meat. "You know how she and Uncle Hyman are about food. Usually their table positively groans with all they serve. Well, help yourselves. I'll put on the water for tea."

"I want another corned beef sandwich," Charlie yelled.

"It's a lucky thing corned beef comes in one big piece. Otherwise we wouldn't have had enough of that either."

"Well, take it easy. Let that be the last," Ella said. "There's hardly anything left."

Someone was at the door. It opened, and a short, stout woman sidled in, her arms piled high with assorted shopping bags. "Hello," she said, looking around uncertainly.

The girls all turned and inspected the newcomer curiously. "My aunt isn't here yet," Ella volunteered politely.

The woman looked puzzled. She gave a quick glance at the door. "You're expecting your aunt?"

"Yes," Henny replied. "Don't go away. She should be here any minute. Here, let me help you with the packages."

"Thank you, but . . ."

Her packages set safely on a chair, the woman folded her arms and regarded the children. "Now tell me, who are you?"

"We're the nieces, and this is the nephew, Charlie," Ella told her.

The woman smiled and gave a nod. "That's nice. I'm pleased to meet you." Then her eyes fell on the table. A look of dismay passed over her face. "Oh, my goodness! I see you ate up the whole supper!"

"I'm awfully sorry," Ella said contritely. "Were you invited too?"

"Who's invited? The supper was for my husband and my son."

"Good gracious!" Henny exclaimed, astonished. "How many people were supposed to eat here tonight?"

"My dear child, you don't understand. The supper was just for the three of us — my husband, my son, and me. After all, this is my apartment."

There was a moment of stunned silence. None of the children could think of anything to say. Finally it was Ella who found her voice. "Your apartment! This is your apartment?"

"Yes, darling," the woman assured her.

"But isn't this apartment 4?" added Sarah.

The woman smiled. "Yes."

"And isn't this the third floor?" Ella asked.

"No. The third floor is downstairs underneath my apartment. This is the fourth floor."

"But how could that be?" Ella asked, confusedly. "We walked up three flights."

"Oh, I see." The woman nodded her head. "You didn't realize that the ground floor is called the first floor. You should have walked up only two flights more."

Ella could feel her cheeks turning scarlet. "Oh, we made such a dreadful mistake! I'm terribly sorry! You see, we thought we were in our aunt's apartment — then we read the note —" she ended lamely.

The woman shrugged her shoulders and chuckled. "Well, it's all right. What's done is done. Don't worry. A mistake can happen."

"But we ate up all your food!" Henny cried.

"Well, as long as you enjoyed it," the woman replied. By now she seemed rather amused.

Slowly the children started edging toward the door. Gertie and Charlotte were the first to slip out. Awkwardly they stood around in the doorway, wanting to get away yet unable to do so.

"We didn't know —" continued Sarah, apologetically.

"We feel just awful," Ella went on. "And you've been so kind about it, too."

As if out of nowhere, Mama and Lena appeared. "What's the matter?" Mama demanded. "Where have you been?"

Lena interrupted. "I was all ready to call the police station. I kept opening the door to see if you were coming. Then we heard your voices, and we came upstairs to see. What are you doing here?"

Everybody began explaining at once. "Oh, Mama!" "Oh,

Lena!" "It was all a big mistake!" "We thought this was your apartment, Lena!"

"Quiet a minute!" Mama ordered. "I don't know what you're saying! Ella, tell me what happened."

Ella looked embarrassed. "Well, Mama, I know it sounds dreadful, but we went into this lady's apartment, and then we ate up her supper."

"The whole supper, Mama!" Gertie burst in. "It was supposed to be for her husband and her son, too."

Bit by bit, with everyone taking part, the whole story came out.

Mama was horrified. "How could you do such a thing?" she scolded. "What happened to your manners? How could you sit down and eat with nobody there?"

"But, Mama, it said in the note we should," Charlotte pleaded.

Mama turned to the woman. "I must apologize for my children. They never did anything like this before, I assure you."

The woman waved it away. "Don't take it to heart. So they ate a supper in my house. What's wrong with that? Believe me, it was a pleasure to see so many nice young faces around my table."

"It was very wrong of them." Mama frowned. "They had no right—"

Lena wouldn't let her finish. She placed a plump arm on Mama's. "Oh, you children! You ate up the lady's supper! Oh, Mama, they ate up the whole supper! Don't you see how funny it is? Oh! Oh! Oh!" She threw back her head and shrieked with laughter. Soon everyone was laughing, and no one was laughing harder than the woman herself.

"Next—time—" she wheezed between gasps, "next time —children—let me know—when you're coming—so I'll prepare enough."

"Well, neighbor," Lena said, wiping her eyes, "what is your name?"

"It's Mrs. Shiner—Molly Shiner."

"This certainly was a comical way for us to meet, Mrs. Shiner. Listen, please. I got plenty food downstairs. Enough for twenty people! Leave another note on the table for your husband and your son and come downstairs with us. Everybody is invited for supper!"

Tea Party

Henny was singing at the top of her voice. "It's a long way to Tipperary. It's a long way to go!"

Ella rattled the bathroom doorknob. "Henny, come on out of there!"

"Why? Don't you like my singing?"

"The singing's fine, but do it outside, please. You're not the only one going out tonight, you know."

"Oh, what's your hurry! You've got plenty of time before that slow-pokey Jules shows up. And besides, I promised Rose I'd come over early."

"I thought you didn't even want to go to her party," Ella said teasingly.

The bathroom door was flung open, and Henny bounced out. The hot, steamy air had tightened her blond hair into curly ringlets, and her impish face was all pink and glowing. "I don't," she retorted, "but the girls are making me! They said if I didn't come, they wouldn't either. So how could I refuse? I don't want to spoil their party!"

"Oh, sure!" Ella replied sarcastically.

Henny went on. "I still don't see why they had to invite boys. It's all that Millie's fault. She started it. We used to have such a lot of fun just by ourselves. Now she's got the whole bunch of girls acting so silly. A party with the *boys*—that's all they talk about! And if you could see the fuss they're making about what they're going to wear! It's positively disgusting!"

Ella grinned.

"What are you doing tonight?" Henny asked casually.

"Nothing special. We'll just go for a walk and maybe stop at an ice-cream parlor."

"Then you won't be needing your white party dress. How about lending it to me?"

Ella's grin vanished. "The answer is no! N - O. NO!"

"Aw, why not? You're not wearing it yourself."

"That doesn't mean I have to lend it to you. You've got your own party dress to wear—your blue one."

"It's all crumpled. I couldn't possibly wear it tonight."

"So iron it!"

"I would, but it's too tight on me. It ripped the last time I wore it. Right under the arm."

"That's not why it ripped, and you know it. It's just that you're very careless. You'll wear my dress just once, and it'll look like a rag. Whatever you wear gets like that."

"Oh, please, Ella! Just this once! I swear I'll never ask for another thing as long as I live!"

"That's what you said the last time."

"But this time I really mean it. Gosh! All the other girls have brand new dresses to wear, and all I have is that old blue thing. Everybody's sick of seeing me in it."

"No. Positively no!"

"Aw, come on. Be nice. I'll be careful with it, I promise. And I'll wash and iron it for you first thing tomorrow."

"It's no use, Henny. You can keep on begging me till doomsday, but this time I'm not giving in."

Henny shrugged her shoulders good-naturedly. "Okay, if that's the way you feel about it." She went off to her room.

Ella watched her go. Now why did she give in so suddenly? she asked herself.

Henny did not really go to her own room. She went, instead, to the tiny hall bedroom which Ella and Sarah shared. Unlike the other bedrooms, this one had a door, always kept locked, which opened on the outside hall. It was this door which interested Henny. With one quick jerk, she slipped the bolt out of its socket and crept back to her own room.

All the while she was bathing, Ella grew more and more remorseful. Why did I have to be so mean? Henny'd look so pretty in my dress, with her gray-green eyes and golden curls.

Meanwhile Henny, in her blue dress, was pirouetting before the family. "How do I look?" she asked.

"Not bad," Mama replied, "but don't you think you should have ironed the dress?"

"I didn't bother, Ma, because I was sure Ella was going to lend me hers."

Mama shook her head. "You're supposed to wear your own dress. Come, take it off. I'll iron it for you."

"But I can't now, Ma. I haven't got time. Rose made me promise I'd be there before the boys come."

Scraps of the conversation came through the bathroom door. That was Henny, Ella told herself, always taking things for granted. No, she steeled herself, she had been quite right not to lend Henny her dress.

"Well, so long, everybody." Henny picked up her coat.

"Have a good time," called Mama.

"What! At a party with boys! It's sure to be a flop!" The door slammed behind her.

The hall carpeting muffled Henny's steps as she tiptoed to the unlocked door of the hall bedroom. Once inside, she threw open the closet door. How beautiful Ella's dress looked! Dazzlingly white and fresh and dainty! It was just begging to be worn. Hurry! Hurry! She tore off her own dress and slipped into Ella's. She wasn't worried about Ella; she was busy in the bathroom. But Sarah might come in any minute, and she always stuck up for Ella. Snatching up her coat and her own dress, she sped down the stairs.

A whisper of conscience pricked at her. You have no right doing this. And what'll you do if Ella finds out? She won't. I'll take good care of it, and I'll put the dress back. She'll never know the difference. Henny shrugged off her uneasiness. I'll worry about it later. She hurried along to Rose's house.

The girls were all gathered in Rose's bedroom by the time Henny arrived. They fluttered about like a flock of giddy birds, primping and turning before the mirror. Heads turned briefly to admire the newcomer. "Henny, you look gorgeous!" "New dress?" Then someone said, "The boys are here already! They all came—every single one of them!"

"Then what are you hanging around in here for?" demanded Henny.

The girls eyed one another. They felt so safe in here, all together like this. To venture out into the parlor where the boys were waiting! Everyone looked at Henny. "Oh, come on!" she cried scornfully. With a toss of her curls, she swept out of the room. The others followed close behind.

The party just couldn't seem to get started. All the boys gathered on one side of the room, the girls on the other. The boys kept laughing uproariously at nothing at all, slapping and pummeling away at one another. "Some party!" Henny said disdainfully. "Everyone standing around doing nothing!"

After a while she became aware of a boy staring at her from across the room. She stared back boldly, till he had to turn his eyes away. Ha! You lost! Henny said to herself, triumphantly. He's got nice twinkly eyes. Nice hair too, black and slicked back. She tugged at Rose's arm. "See that fellow over there? I'm going over and introduce myself."

"No, Henny, you mustn't!"

"Why not?"

"A girl's supposed to wait until the boy comes over to her, that's why. He'll think you're awfully fresh."

"Well, somebody's got to make the first move."

A second later she was staring down at Mr. Slick Hair. "Hello. I'm Henrietta—Henny for short."

The boy jumped to his feet. "My name—er—is Ed," he stammered, his face turning red. Sheepishly he put out his hand. But he seemed glad she'd come over. Henny could tell. Somehow she felt glad too. "Come on," she cried gaily, "introduce me to your friends."

"She didn't want us to invite boys. Now look at her!" Millie said hotly to Rose. "Picks out the best-looking one in the whole room."

"Why didn't you go over yourself?" Rose retorted. "Nobody stopped you."

In a little while boys and girls were jabbering away together. Some grouped themselves around the player piano and sang the latest songs. Soon a new roll of dance music was inserted into the piano, and a few adventurous couples swung into a foxtrot.

The girls could tell right off that the boys hadn't had much practice. They kept stepping all over the girls' feet. Quickly Henny took over. Running from one boy to another, she gave them dancing lessons right then and there. Her manner was so friendly and gay that none of the boys seemed to mind. They appeared to be enjoying themselves immensely.

Afterward, when each boy had had his chance, Henny sat down on the sofa and waved her handkerchief before her flushed face. "Am I hot!" she cried. Instantly half a dozen boys rushed to fetch her a cool drink.

Henny was having a fine time. The boys hovered about talking and joking with her as if they had been friends forever. But all the while, she was pleasantly aware that the attractive Ed kept looking at her.

"She's so popular," a girl commented enviously.

"Why shouldn't she be?" Rose said. "She's so lively and so much fun. And she's pretty."

"Aw, she's just a big show-off!" Millie said with malice. "Look at the way she's making up to that Edward."

"You're just jealous, Millie," Rose answered promptly.

A sudden commotion interrupted Millie's reply. Someone had found a piece of rope, and a game of tug-of-war was in progress. Three boys in a line pulled at one end of the rope— and there was Henny, with Ed and another boy, holding fast to the other.

"And that's not showing off, I suppose," sneered Millie. "Tomboy!"

Straining and grunting, the contestants pulled away. "Come on, you lazybones! Pull!" The line swayed, now this way, now that. "You'll break something for sure!" Rose cried out, worried. Inch by inch, Henny's side seemed to be gaining. A sudden fierce tug and the line swerved against the refreshment table. "Hey, watch out!" Rose screamed. Slam! Bang! Bump! The cake dishes rattled, the glasses danced crazily, and the tall pitcher of iced tea rocked. Sw-a-ssh! A shower of tea and lemon slices splashed over the tablecloth and down to the floor. The startled players piled up in a heap.

Rose surveyed the mess in dismay. "It's a lucky thing my

ma is out getting the ice cream. She'd have a fit if she saw this! Quick, everybody, let's clean up before she gets back!"

In no time at all the floor was mopped, and the table set to rights. Rose refilled the pitcher with more iced tea.

"Look!" Millie pointed at Henny. "Look what you did to yourself!"

Henny glanced down. Big splotches of tea stains were spread across Ella's party dress. In a panic, she dashed off to the kitchen, with Rose at her heels.

First they tried washing it with plain water, then soap and water. No use; the stains stood out more vividly than before. "We're just making it worse," Henny said ruefully.

"Gosh, Henny, what are you going to do?"

"I don't know," Henny replied, with a sinking feeling. She slumped into a chair. "The worst part of it is, this is Ella's dress. I never should have come. Then it wouldn't have happened."

"But if you hadn't come, you wouldn't have met Ed."

Henny didn't answer; she was too upset.

Rose went on talking. "He's the youngest one in his class, but he gets the highest marks."

"How old is he?"

"He'll be fifteen in January."

Henny stared at Rose in disbelief. "Fifteen! Why, that's six months younger than me! He's nothing but a baby! Can you beat that! Wasting my time with a baby! And I thought he was so nice, too!"

She felt angry—at Ed—at everybody! Girls were stupid, anyway, making such a fuss over a bunch of silly boys! To think that for this she had to go and ruin Ella's beautiful dress! She snapped at Rose. "You can tell the girls for me, they're welcome to Ed. They can have him for a present!"

Once more she fell to examining the tea-stained frock. It was absolutely hopeless trying to wash out tea stains, she realized desperately. Why, even when Mama wanted ecru-colored curtains instead of white, she always dyed them with tea . . .

"I ought to go back, Henny," Rose was saying apologetically. "After all, it is my party."

Henny made a sudden grab for her. A thought had struck her like lightning—dyed them with tea. "No, Rose! Wait a minute! I've got an idea! But I'll need your help!"

"All right. What do you want me to do?"

"Get me lots and lots of tea!" Henny exclaimed.

Rose looked at her blankly. "Tea? What for?"

"I'm going to stain the dress."

"Are you crazy! Look what the tea did already!"

"That's just it! Instead of having tea stains in different places, I'll stain it all over!"

"But what good will that do? It won't be white. It'll be sort of tan."

Henny waved her hands gleefully. "Ecru, you mean!"

"What about Ella? What'll she say?"

"It's better to have an ecru dress than a stained white one. Come on, we're just wasting time. Start making lots and lots of tea! And hurry!"

It wasn't long before they were both bent over the wash tub. Clad in Rose's bathrobe, Henny lowered the party dress into the strong tea solution. They watched intently as the golden color seeped through the floating whiteness.

"Think it'll come out all right?" Rose queried nervously.

Henny wasn't too sure, but she made her voice sound confident. " 'Course it will!"

Slowly she kept swishing the dress around. The minutes ticked by. "Better take it out," Rose cautioned. "It'll get so dark it'll look more like coffee."

"Oh, stop worrying!" Henny took a deep breath. "Well, here goes!" She held the dress up high out of the water.

Rose put her hands over her eyes. "I'm too scared to look!"

Anxiously Henny examined the dress, first on one side,

then on the other. "It's perfect!" She laughed aloud in delighted relief. "What did I tell you?" Simply perfect!"

Rose's hands dropped away from her face. "It is! Thank heavens! I swear, Henny, one of these days you're going to scare me to death!"

Next they hung the dripping dress on the line outside the kitchen window. "Lucky there's a nice breeze blowing," Henny said happily. "It's such thin material it'll be ready for ironing in no time."

The kitchen door opened, and in came Rose's mother with the ice cream. "What happened to you?" she asked the bathrobed Henny.

"Oh, we spilt things. My dress got all wet."

"That's a shame! But Rose can lend you one of hers meanwhile. We don't want you to miss the party. I'll iron the dress for you as soon as it's dry."

"Oh, thanks an awful lot," Henny replied gratefully.

The rest of the evening was very gay. Rose's mother brought in ice cream and cake, and the young people ate till not a speck was left. Everybody agreed that the party was a huge success. When the time came for good-bys, they hated to leave. And no one was more reluctant than Henny.

Rose's mother had ironed the dress beautifully. "It's such a pretty dress!" she remarked as she turned it over to Henny.

I only hope Ella thinks so, Henny prayed as she walked home with the gang.

At her doorstep, she bade them all a hearty good night and crept stealthily up the stairs. She stopped on the landing. Everything was quiet, but a streak of light glimmered at the sill of the kitchen door. Mama must be waiting up for her. Quickly she changed into her own blue dress. She slung Ella's dress over her arm and covered it up carefully with her coat. She opened the door.

"Well, Henny," Mama looked up from her knitting, "did you have a good time?"

"Oh, it was all right."

"Yes? Well, it's late. You'll tell us all about it tomorrow. Better go straight to bed. Ella's asleep already."

As Mama went to lock the door, Henny slid past and hurried into her room. She hung Ella's dress up in her own closet, tidily smoothing out any wrinkles. Tomorrow morning it would be back in Ella's closet.

It was the following Sunday. Jules had invited Ella to a dance downtown. Ella looked forward to it keenly. It would be nice to visit the old neighborhood and meet many of her friends again. She hummed to herself as she dressed.

In the parlor, Henny was crawling over the floor with Charlie on her back. "Giddyap horsie!" Charlie shouted.

Ella's humming came to an abrupt halt. "Where's my white dress? I can't find it! And what's this?"

The astonished exclamations could be heard in the parlor. The horsie stopped giddyapping and listened.

"That must be your dress." Sarah sounded equally perplexed. "Only it's a different color. Ooh, it's beautiful!"

"The color is gorgeous!" cried Charlotte.

"So creamy looking!" agreed Gertie.

The horsie, with Charlie still on her back, poked her head into the bedroom.

Ella held up her dress. "Look, Henny. Look what happened to my white dress!"

Henny just stared.

"Must be something in the material," Gertie said.

"Maybe it's from the new camphor balls we put in the closets," offered Charlotte.

Ella shook her head in puzzlement. "I just can't understand it. I know white turns yellowish if you don't put bluing in the water. But I've never seen anything like this. Let's show it to Mama."

"Mmmm! It certainly is peculiar," Mama said.

Henny's heart went thumpety-thump. Was Mama looking at her?

"Well, anyway, the color is lovely," declared Sarah. "I like it better than when it was plain white."

"So do I," echoed Charlotte and Gertie.

Only Ella was doubtful. "You think so? I don't know. What do you think, Henny?"

Henny found it difficult to answer. "I think it's nice. And you know how boys are. Jules'll think it's a brand new dress."

"Come, Ella, try it on," Mama said.

So Ella put on the dress, and the whole family ohed and ahed in admiration.

The bell rang. "That's Jules!" Ella flew to open the door.

Jules entered, looking very handsome in a navy-blue suit, with a brand-new straw hat under one arm.

"Hello, Jules. How are you?" The family greetings showered down upon him.

"Thank you. I'm fine," he replied very politely. He stood stiffly by the parlor door, fumbling with a long, thin tissue-paper package.

"You look so nice in your new suit, Jules," Ella said.

"I always say if a man doesn't look good in a navy-blue

suit, then he just wouldn't look good in anything," Mama remarked.

Jules smiled in embarrassment. "Here, Ella," he said, thrusting his package into her hands. "I think this will look nice on your dress. It's the prettiest dress I've ever seen."

Ella unwrapped the tissue paper as the girls all pressed close to see. Out came a single red rose. "Oh, it's lovely, Jules. Just lovely!" Ella exclaimed.

Jules grinned. "Some day, when I'm rich, I'll buy you dozens and dozens of them."

Jules and Ella had long since gone. The younger children had just been sent to bed. Now Mama, without saying a word, took hold of Henny's arm and led her firmly into her own bedroom. Shutting the door, she turned and said very quietly, "All right, Henny. Now let's hear all about it. No dress ever got that color by itself."

Henny squirmed unhappily. Her voice was low. "I made it that color, Ma. I dyed it. With tea."

"That's what I figured," Mama said. "But why?"

"I had to, Mama. It got all splashed with tea at Rose's party. It looked a mess—all stained up."

"How did this happen?"

Henny couldn't bear to look at Mama. This was going to be the hardest part of all to tell—how she had lied and stolen Ella's dress.

"Well, Henny!" Mama prompted.

Shamefacedly, Henny told the whole story. "I feel terrible, Ma. I know it was a mean thing to do. I wanted to tell Ella about it a hundred times—but I just couldn't get started."

Mama looked very severe. "It was very bad, and I expect you to own up to Ella and ask her to forgive you. I know you didn't deliberately intend to be wicked, but the dress was not yours. Lucky for you the color came out right."

"It sure did, Ma, didn't it?" Henny said hopefully.

Mama regarded her sternly. "And now, Henny," she continued, "since you're such an experienced washer, you'll do the entire family wash this week. It's still early, so you can start by soaking the clothes right now. And there is a pair of parlor curtains that need dipping in tea. So you'll do those also."

Henny made no protest. She went straight to work. It was so good to have the whole thing out in the open. As she leaned over the washtubs, churning the clothes in the soapy water, she sighed happily. Somehow it was as if her wrongdoings were being washed away too.

Ella Takes Over

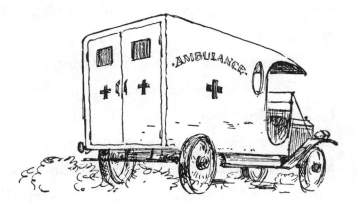

"Dee-dul! Dee-dul!" Charlie sang as he trailed his stick along the foyer wall. "Dee-dul, dee-dul!" Down the length of one wall the stick rode, until at last it came to the open door leading into the dining room. Charlie's bright smiling face peeped around the edge. "I go dee-dul all the way!" he announced, and immediately started the stick on its interesting journey again.

"He's so little he doesn't even realize Mama is sick," Gertie said, sniffling.

Ella held up a warning finger. "You mustn't cry, Gertie. We don't want Mama to see us upset."

"But I can't—help it. The tears—just—keep on coming."

Charlotte put her arms around Gertie. "Put your fingers on your eyes and press hard . . . and take big swallows. That'll hold the tears back."

"Afterwards we can cry," Sarah whispered.

The downstairs bell rang loud and long. "I wanna tick back!" yelled Charlie, dropping his stick and racing madly into the kitchen. He stood under the buzzer, hopping up and down to reach it. Henny picked him up, and his eager fingers pressed hard on the little round button. "I pressed it!" Charlie announced, pleased with himself. He rushed back to his dee-dul game.

Papa came out of the bedroom. "That must be the ambulance. They came very fast," he said.

How tired he looks, Ella thought. She longed to put her arms around him to comfort him.

"Go in to Mama now, children, and tell her good-by," Papa said. He paused briefly. "Be careful!"

Mrs. Healy, their landlady, who lived downstairs, was standing at Mama's bedside. Mama lay still in her bed, one arm across her face. "Mama," Ella called softly. Slowly the arm came down. Mama turned her head and scanned the faces of her children, smiling wanly. "How are you ever going to get along?" she whispered in a troubled voice.

Ella spoke confidently. "Now, don't you worry, Ma. I'll take care of everything. Don't forget, I'm almost seventeen—practically a grownup!"

"It's going to be hard," Mama said.

"We'll help, Mama. We'll all work," the sisters chimed in.

"You'll see," added Papa. "They'll do an A-1, first-class job. After all, they have such a wonderful teacher."

"Why, sure, there's nothing to fret about," Mrs. Healy said heartily. "These children of yours are okay. Besides, I'm right downstairs. They can always count on me to help out."

"Thank you, Mrs. Healy," Mama replied gratefully. "You're a good, kind neighbor." A spasm of pain made her turn her head to the wall.

Papa let the hospital attendants in. Swiftly they bundled Mama in a blanket and lifted her onto the stretcher.

Charlie came running over. "Mama's getting a ride!" he cried, skipping alongside the stretcher.

"My sweet little Charlie," Mama murmured.

The family followed the stretcher down the stairs and out into the July sunshine where the ambulance stood waiting.

"I wanna ride in the car with Mama!" Charlie clamored.

Papa picked him up and held him close.

The ambulance began moving away from the curb, its warning bell clanging shrilly. Panic seized Charlie. "Mama!" he screamed. "Don' go away, Mama! Don' go away!"

He beat at Papa with his little fists. "I wanna go with Mama!" With a sudden twist, he tore free of Papa and began to run after the ambulance.

"Charlie, come back here!" Henny yelled. Ella caught hold of Charlie's arm, but he wrenched himself loose and kept on running.

Soon the ambulance had disappeared in the distance. Charlie came to a halt. He looked around despairingly. He felt lost and helpless. He began to weep bitterly.

Papa knelt down and held out his arms. "Charlie, Charlie," he said brokenly. "Mama's coming back soon."

Charlie would not be comforted. He turned his back on Papa, wailing aloud his unhappiness.

Charlie ran to Henny. She picked him up, and he buried his face in her shoulder. With heavy hearts, the family went slowly back to the house.

All the while, Mrs. Healy's daughter, Grace, had stood silently by on the low stoop. Now she came toward them. Gently she stroked Charlie's hair. "Poor little boy," she murmured. Suddenly she turned and ran into the house. She was back in no time. "Look, Charlie!" she cried. "Look what I've got!"

Charlie peeked over Henny's shoulder. There was something in Grace's arms. His tear-streaked face came up slowly. He stared at the small furry ball curled up against Grace's chest. "It's a kitty! A baby kitty!" Grace continued coaxingly. Between sobs, Charlie's hand reached out timidly to touch the gray softness. The kitty's small pink mouth opened, and it mewed.

"He talks . . . he talks when I pet him," Charlie said in surprise. "Can I hold him?"

"Uh-huh. But you'll have to be careful. He's so little."

"I be careful . . . I be very careful," Charlie promised.

So Henny set him down, and he held out his arms to receive the precious kitty. Then, gravely he walked to the stoop and sat down. Cradling the kitty, he cooed tenderly to it. "Don' be scared, kitty—don' cry. Mama's coming back."

The kitty snuggled down contentedly. And though he still shuddered now and then from all the weeping, the little boy seemed contented too.

"Thank you, Grace," Papa said. He turned to the children. "I must go to the hospital now."

"Can't we go with you?" pleaded Gertie.

Papa shook his head. "They don't allow children under sixteen, so only Ella could come. But Ella, you must stay with the children."

"Yes, Papa."

"The operation may take a long time. So don't get frightened if you see it's getting late and I'm not back. So far you've been fine, brave children. And that's the way Mama and I want you should go on being. Of course an appendix operation is serious. But we got the doctor in time."

"Call me the minute you have news," suggested Mrs. Healy.

"You're sure you won't mind?"

"Of course not. What's my telephone for?"

"Thanks, Mrs. Healy," Papa said earnestly. "Thank you for everything. Well, I'd better go now."

They watched him walk away, his shoulders bowed, his steps heavy. Now there was no Papa either.

Gertie clung to Charlotte. "But people die from operations! Do you think—"

"Don't say it." Charlotte frowned. "Don't even think such a thing!"

Ella thought: It's up to me now. I have to take Mama's place. What would Mama do at such a time? "I know how we can take some of the worry away from Mama," she said aloud.

"How?"

"By going right upstairs and straightening out the house and getting dinner. Who wants to come with me?"

"Me! Me, too!" Everybody was eager to pitch in.

Mrs. Healy beamed. "Good girls!" She turned to her daughter. "Grace, go along and give them a hand."

Upstairs, the girls set to work with a will. Ella and Grace made beds and swept. Charlotte and Gertie dusted. Sarah did the dishes, and Henny let Charlie help her mop up the kitchen and bathroom floors. "I've got to keep him out from under everybody's feet," she explained.

As they went about their tasks, each one tried hard not to show how miserable and anxious she felt. They tried to speak of other things, but they could not keep Mama out of their minds. After a while they just stopped trying.

In Mama's room, Ella and Grace were smoothing out the spread on the bed. Ella's hands moved slower and slower. She began to speak, almost as if she were thinking aloud. "Mama's never been away from us before. I guess that's why we're all so disturbed. Before, no matter what happened to any of us, there was always Mama to turn to. Mama's so strong—like a mountain! No matter how hard we lean on her, we know she won't topple. Now the mountain isn't here.

"The little ones—they have to lean on somebody. And with Papa away all day, it'll be me. But what about me? Who will I lean on? I guess this is what growing up really means, Grace. Standing on your own two feet and being your own mountain."

Grace came around the bed to her reassuringly. "Maybe you don't know it, but you're quite a little rock yourself, even if you're no bigger than a minute. Besides," she went on, "you're not all alone. There's your Papa and your relatives.

And then there's my father and mother—all glad to help. And then don't forget me! I've got a big shoulder you can cry on if you ever have to."

Ella smiled at her friend. "If only my Aunt Lena were here," she said. "She'd be such a help. But Uncle Hyman has already rented a tiny place in the Catskills for the summer. You see, my aunt's going to have a baby."

She sighed. "Nothing ever works out the way you plan. I was supposed to start work today in my Uncle Joe's place. Twelve dollars a week! I could have earned enough this summer to carry me through the whole year. I hate to have to keep asking Papa for money."

She gave herself a little shake. "I'm setting a fine example, standing around gabbing instead of working. Nobody ate much for lunch today. I think I ought to try to get the kids to eat something."

Soon a big pot of cocoa was steaming on the range. Ella coaxed the youngsters to the table, and everyone sat around sipping the hot drink and nibbling on soda crackers. All the while, eyes kept straying to the clock on the kitchen shelf, ears kept listening for Mrs. Healy's call. Gertie voiced aloud what they were all thinking. "It's such a long, long time. Why doesn't Papa call?"

"Watching the clock only makes it seem longer," Ella said quietly. "Look, why don't you all go downstairs till suppertime? It's so nice out. You can stay near the house, and I'll let you know the minute Mrs. Healy calls. Go ahead," she urged, "I'll wash the dishes myself."

"Well, I guess it's about time I went down," Grace decided. She squeezed Ella's hand. "See you later, Ella. And don't worry," she whispered.

Ella washed the dishes, cleaned the sink, and wrung out the dishcloth and hung it up to dry. The house was unbearably quiet. Slowly the clock kept ticking away. How much longer would they have to wait? Could something have gone wrong? Her heart began to pound with a dreadful fear. Oh, Papa, please, please call, she prayed silently.

Maybe she should call the hospital. Mrs. Healy would let her use the phone. Yes, that's what she'd do. She opened the door and hurried down the stairs.

As she reached the first floor, she halted abruptly. Gertie, Charlotte, and Sarah were sitting in a forlorn group on the bottom steps. "What are you doing here?" Ella demanded.

"We can hear the phone from here," replied Charlotte.

"It rang twice already," Gertie added tearfully. "But each time—it was somebody else."

Ella couldn't find it in her heart to scold. She just sat down and waited with them.

The telephone rang again. The children sprang to their feet. Let it be Papa this time, Ella wished fervently. They waited, straining their ears to catch the conversation. The minutes seemed like years. At last the door opened, and Mrs. Healy and Grace were beckoning them in. "Everything's all right," Mrs. Healy cried joyfully. "Your Mama's fine. Come on! Your Papa's still on the phone. He wants to speak to you."

"Get Henny, quick!" Ella yelled to Sarah, as she rushed to the phone.

"Never mind, Sarah. I'll get her," Grace offered.

In another moment, Grace was back, with Henny and Charlie in tow. Breathless with excitement, they dashed into the Healy parlor.

Clustered around the Healy phone, the children piled excitedly on top of one another, each trying to shout into the telephone at the same time. To Papa, it must have sounded like a lot of jibber-jabber. But they could hear his laughter flowing back over the wire. The children's answering laughter exploded like popcorn in all directions. Mama was safe!

Sabbath Without Mama

The warm sun shone on Sarah's face, and she opened her eyes. "Oh, I'm so glad it's today instead of yesterday," she said, stretching contentedly.

Ella smiled. "Yes, it's a wonderful feeling to know that Mama will be all right." She jumped out of bed and ran through the rooms. "Wake up, everybody! Let's get breakfast!"

Breakfast over, Ella rapped on the table with her spoon. "Listen, everybody," she declared. "I think we ought to have a schedule."

"That's a swell idea," agreed Sarah.

"What's a schedule?" Gertie asked.

"It's a list of things you plan to do. It'll show all the jobs and who does what and when. You'll see when we draw it up."

Dishes were stacked in the sink and beds went unmade while the girls struggled over the schedule. Even Charlie got into the spirit of it. Lying on his tummy on the floor, he imitated his sisters, scribble-scrabbling all over a big sheet of paper.

"Let's tackle the big jobs first," Ella began. "Now, let's see. Mondays we'll wash."

"Who's we?" inquired Henny.

"We means all of us." Ella was emphatic. "Of course," she went on, "big things like sheets and tablecloths go to the wet wash laundry. They'll still have to be dried and ironed at home, but at least we won't have the job of washing them."

So they went on straight through the week, marking down the days for things like ironing, polishing furniture, window cleaning, marketing, and so on. When it was finally finished, Henny took one look at the crowded list and let out a howl. "You've got enough things there to keep us working twenty-four hours a day! When do we rest?"

Ella pointed to Saturday. "There! The Sabbath! That's the day of rest, remember?"

Henny grinned. "Thank goodness for that!"

"I know it seems like an awful lot to do," Ella went on,

"but you know what Mama always says—do your work with good will, and it'll get done twice as fast. You'll see, there'll be lots of time left. Mama manages, and she's only one."

"Besides, Henny, think of all the practice you'll be getting," Sarah added. "When you get married, you'll know how to do everything."

"Who needs practice!" scoffed Henny. "I'm going to marry a millionaire and have a different servant for every job."

"Oh, sure," Ella commented dryly. She chewed on her pencil. "Somebody will have to spend a good deal of time with Charlie. He needs a lot of care—bathing him, staying with him outdoors, putting him to bed."

"I'll do it," volunteered Henny.

"Oh, that's swell, Henny," Ella replied gratefully. "You're good with him. Better than any of us."

Ella tacked the schedule up on the kitchen door. "That's settled. Now, let's get to work."

For the next few days things ran very smoothly. The schedule seemed to be working out just fine. Papa asked Ella to make him a copy. "I want to show it to Mama," he said proudly. As for Mrs. Healy, when she first saw it, she laughed heartily. "I ought to have you make one up for me. Maybe then Grace would take more interest in my housework."

"But, Mrs. Healy," Charlotte exclaimed, "she's always coming up here to help us!"

Grace looked at her mother and laughed. "Well, it's so jolly up here. With everybody pitching in, it just doesn't seem like work."

On Friday morning, when Mrs. Healy and Grace looked in on the family, they found the kitchen as busy as an anthill. "This will be our first Friday night without Mama," Ella explained. "We want to have everything as nice as when Mama is home. Only there are a million things to do! We'll never get done!"

"Perhaps I can help," Mrs. Healy said. "Sarah, what are you fighting with in the chopping bowl?"

"We're making gefüllte fish."

"Well, I can't help you out with that," Mrs. Healy said. "I never even tasted it, let alone made it."

"I've never made it either," confessed Ella. "But it belongs on Friday night. I have the recipe, of course, but I only hope it turns out all right. If it does, we'll bring you some."

Gertie and Charlotte were sitting on the floor beneath the open window, busily polishing the brassware. Spread out before them on a large sheet of newspaper were all the assorted pieces which added such lustre to Mama's kitchen. "You two seem to be getting along all right," Mrs. Healy said, "but why on the floor?"

"The polish smells awful, so Ella said we have to keep away from the food," replied Charlotte.

"I've only asked them a dozen times to go out into the hall or into the dining room, but they won't," Ella added. "Afraid they'll miss something."

"Where's Charlie?" Mrs. Healy asked Henny, who was busy shelling peas.

A curly blond head peeked out from under the table. "Here I am. I'm hiding. An' the kitty's hiding too."

The head disappeared. Immediately assorted meows and scuffling erupted from under the table cover. Henny ducked under the table. A moment later she came crawling out, the kitten in her arms, with a protesting Charlie scrambling after.

Henny stroked the kitten. "Poor little thing." She turned to Charlie. "How would you like it if I pulled your tail?" she scolded.

"I pulled it only a little bit." Charlie pouted. "An' anyway, I haven't got no tail."

"You do that once more, and I'll spank you right where the tail would be."

At the sink, Ella was sprinkling coarse salt in large handfuls over some uncooked meat. "Ella," Grace cried, aghast. "What are you doing! You'll burn everyone's mouth off with all that salt!"

Ella smiled. "It gets washed off later. This is how we make our meat kosher."

"Oh, that's how it's done," Mrs. Healy said. "I've always wondered."

"That's only part of it. First you have to soak the meat in cold water for half an hour. Then you wash it off. Next you sprinkle salt all over the meat and place it on a wooden board set on a slant so that the meat can drain freely. After an hour, you rinse it three times in cold water. Then it's kosher and ready for cooking."

"It's quite a job preparing your meat," Mrs. Healy said.

"Yes," agreed Henny. "You spend hours fixing it, and then the whole thing is gobbled up in a couple of minutes."

"Mrs. Healy," Ella said, "there is one thing you can help me with."

"Sure. And what's that?"

"Well," Ella went on, "I'm not even trying to bake our own *challis* for the Sabbath like Mama does. I'll buy those at the bakery. But I would just love to bake a coffeecake. We always have one for breakfast on Saturday. Papa loves it."

"Then what are we waiting for?" Mrs. Healy said, rolling up her sleeves.

They went to work, and soon the dough was set to rise in a pan on the back of the stove. "I've got to go down and attend to my own cooking," Mrs. Healy told Ella, "but when the dough has risen to twice its size, you call me. Come, Grace, this gives me an idea. We'll make a coffeecake too."

The preparations went swiftly. Now the soup was on and the meat ready for roasting. Ella took down the box of matches from the kitchen shelf.

"Lemme light it! Lemme!" Charlie cried.

"No!" Ella answered firmly. "It's too dangerous. But you can blow out the match afterward."

Charlie watched Ella strike the match against the side of the box. It was ablaze! Charlie was silent with the wonder of it. Just a second ago it had been a mere stick. Now suddenly and gloriously it had flamed alive! How it glowed! He felt all jumpy with excitement. If only the brightness would last forever! But now Ella was saying, "Well, Charlie. Blow it! Blow it out!"

He puckered his lips and blew. Solemnly he regarded the charred bit that remained in Ella's hand. Why wouldn't his mean sisters let him light matches? They did it all the time.

There was the whole boxful on the window sill where Ella had left them. Swiftly Charlie snatched it up and skipped out of the room. Everyone was so busy that no one noticed. Henny, with one ear cocked, could hear Charlie singing happily in Mama's room. Everything was all right.

Charlie went over to the window and set the precious box down on the sill. Now it was all his to play with! Eagerly, he pulled out a match and scratched it against the sandpapery side of the box. He clutched it so tightly the slender stick snapped. Charlie frowned. "No good!" He tossed the pieces out of the window.

He took a second match. He scraped and scraped, and pretty soon the red and blue tip was all gone. "More no good!" The second match followed the first through the window.

Puzzled, he tried a third one. It burst into flame! His eyes opened wide as he contemplated the magical brightness. All too soon it was burning itself out—it was almost down to his fingers! Quickly he brought another match to it. What a lovely spurty sound it made as it caught fire!

Through the open window, the soft summer breeze pulled fitfully at the crisp white curtains. It occurred so swiftly, Charlie scarcely knew what happened. The flame made a jump toward the curtain and ran up its length.

Frightened, Charlie backed away, the match stump still in his hand. He watched, fascinated, as the curtain seemed to melt away. A little puff of wind snatched up the last bit of lacy whiteness and sent it spinning like a flaming top down to the yard below.

Charlie tiptoed over to the window and peered over the ledge. There was nothing there. He looked up at the bare rod. There was nothing there either—nothing at all! He spread his arms out in a helpless gesture. "All gone!" he announced. Only some ashy specks on the window sill remained. He blew at them and shooed them out. Then he stepped back and studied the window again. He stood very still, his small rounded tummy pushed forward. The window has no clothes on, he decided. What would Mama say when she saw that? She'd be awfully angry. She might even give him a spanking!

But Mama wasn't here. She was sick in the hospital. Ella was here. She could spank! His eyes went darting round the room. The bed! That was a fine hiding place! Quickly he crawled under. He was safe in his own snug little den.

"Charlie must be up to something. It's much too quiet in there," Henny said in the kitchen. "I'd better take a look. Charlie!" she called out. "Charlie, where are you?"

Charlie's heart went bumpety-bump. It mustn't do that. It

must be still as a mouse, like himself.

Henny's voice was coming nearer. Now she was in the bedroom. He could see her shoes coming and going. All at once the shoes halted. "What in the world! Hey, Ella—everybody, come in here quick!" Henny yelled.

The startled sisters came running. Henny pointed to the window. "Where's the curtain?"

"What could have happened to it?" Ella asked, wonderingly.

"Maybe it fell out," Gertie said.

Sarah and Henny hung over the window ledge. No curtain down there.

Ella's brows puckered into a frown. "The rod's still up there. The curtain couldn't have fallen down. Someone's taken it off!" She studied the sisters' faces suspiciously.

"Oh, don't be silly!" Henny told her. "Why should we want to do that? Maybe it's Charlie. He might have torn it off somehow. Where is the little rascal, anyway?"

Charlie hardly dared breathe. He flattened his nose against the floor.

"Charlie!" the girls called. They ran all through the house searching for him. "Maybe he went downstairs," suggested Charlotte. "He could have gone through the parlor."

"With the curtain?" asked Sarah.

"Why not?" answered Henny. "He—"

Just then Charlie's nose tickled. He sneezed—a tiny ker-choo! Instantly five girls were down by the bed. Five hands poked under the bedspread. There was the culprit! Henny pulled him out by his heels. Immediately he was surrounded by a forest of accusing fingers. "What have you been up to?" "Where's the curtain?" "Why are you hiding?"

"Shush, all of you!" Henny silenced her sisters. She made her voice very gentle. "Nobody's going to hurt you, Charlie," she said calmly. "Just tell us what happened!"

In a sudden flood of tears, Charlie blubbered out the whole story. The girls looked at one another, shaken. "You must never, never play with matches!" they kept repeating over and over again.

"It's really all my fault," Ella reproached herself afterward. "I had no business leaving the matches where he could get at them."

When Papa heard about it later that evening, he declared, "The angels in heaven are watching over my children with extra special care because they know Mama isn't here."

Twilight had come. Now was the moment to welcome the Sabbath. With no Mama there, it was Ella who sang the blessing over the candles.

Praised be Thou, O Lord our God, King of the Universe, Who has sanctified with His commandments, and commanded us to kindle the Sabbath lights.

Listening to the familiar prayer, the children felt drawn close together in peace and love and understanding. Once again the reverent spirit of the Sabbath was upon them.

Happily they awaited Papa's return from synagogue. He would smile upon them. He would be so pleased with all they had done.

And then Papa came home. "Good Sabbath," he said quietly as he opened the door. "Good Sabbath," they replied, and stood in line to receive his blessing.

They waited expectantly for some word of praise, but he said nothing. He just washed his hands and sat down at the head of the table. "Charlie," he said, drawing his son onto his lap, "do you know that every Friday night, two angels walk home with Papa when he leaves the synagogue?"

Charlie's eyes grew big. "Two angels!" he repeated.

"Yes," said Papa, "a good angel and a bad angel, and they walk on each side of the Papa. The good angel is dressed all in white, and he is very beautiful, because he has a kind and loving face. The bad angel is dressed all in black, and you would not like to look at him, for his face is very ugly—dark with anger all the time.

"Now, when the Papa reaches his house, he goes inside alone. The angels stay outside, but they peep in the windows to see how things are. If the house is clean and bright and the family all dressed up in their nice Sabbath clothes; if the candle-sticks are shining and the candles are lit; if the table is nicely set; then the good angel feels so happy he wants to jump for joy. He smiles a big smile, and he says, 'May all your Sabbaths be so bright and cheerful.' At this, the bad angel gets very cross, and his ugly face grows even darker with anger. But there is nothing he can do about it, and so, even though he doesn't want to, he has to give in. He has to say 'Amen. So be it!'

"Now, if the house is not clean, and the candles are not lit; if the table is not laid with shining dishes, and everybody is sitting around in the same clothes they wore all day, then it is the bad angel who is overjoyed. His mean little eyes glisten in his wicked face, and he rubs his hands together gleefully, and he says, 'So may all your Sabbaths be!'

"And the poor good angel is sad. He weeps, and the tears run down his cheeks. But still he has to say 'Amen. So be it!' "

Papa's wide, gentle smile turned full upon all his children. "Charlie, which angel do you think is the happy one tonight?"

"The good angel, Papa! The good angel!" Charlie cried.

"That's right, Charlie," said Papa, and the girls' hearts swelled with pride.

Charlie slipped off Papa's lap and ran to the window, his eyes searching the darkness outside. "I don't see the angels,

Papa. Why can't I see the angels?" he asked, disappointedly.

"Only God can see the angels," Papa said softly. "But they are there all right. Listen hard, Charlie, and maybe you will hear the beating of their wings as they fly away. Ssh-ssh!"

Charlie listened with all his might. He lifted a rapt face to Papa. "I can hear them, Papa," he whispered.

Dining Out

On Sunday Jules came calling. "How's Mama?" he inquired.

Papa peered at him over the top of his newspaper. "Mama's coming along fine, thank you."

"That's great! Look, Ella, I've been thinking," Jules went on. "You've been working pretty hard. You deserve a change. Tonight you're going to have supper with me in a restaurant."

"In a restaurant! Oh, boy!" Henny exclaimed. "I've always wanted to eat in a restaurant!"

"Well—I—" Jules gestured helplessly as if to give the whole thing up.

"You ninny!" Ella whispered fiercely in Henny's ear. "He

doesn't mean the whole family. He means *me!*"

"Oh, pardon me, Jules, my error," Henny said airily.

Ella turned to Papa. "Will it be all right, Papa?"

"Yes, yes. Go ahead. Have a good time. Maybe, for once, we will manage without you."

"Thanks, Papa," Ella cried. She twirled about. "Am I dressed properly, Jules?"

"Certainly. You look swell."

"All right, then. I'll be with you in a minute. I'll just get my hat."

She dashed into her room, took a final look in the mirror, and dabbed her nose furiously with some of Mama's rice powder. She was tingling with excitement. Eating in a restaurant was such a grown-up thing to do! She wondered what it would be like.

"We'll take the subway down to 59th Street and walk from there," Jules said, as they left the house.

Half an hour later they were strolling hand in hand along Broadway. Overhead, huge electric lights flashed on and off. On theater marquees, rows of blinking bulbs lighted up bright colored posters. It was thrilling to be part of the gay crowd that thronged the streets. This is the enchanted world of adults, Ella thought, and now I belong to it, too.

There seemed to be a great many restaurants to choose from. Jules kept stopping uncertainly every so often saying, "I just want to look it over." At several places, he stared for some time through the windows, but made no move to go in. "It's got to be exactly the right kind of place, you know," he observed firmly.

Ella grew a little nervous. I hope he doesn't pick a place that's too fancy. Oh, maybe we should have stayed home, and I could have made supper for all of us. It would have been so much more comfortable.

"Here we are," Jules suddenly announced. With a flourish, he held open the door for her.

As she stepped in, Ella stumbled slightly. Oh, dear, how awkward!

Gallantly, Jules caught her arm and squeezed it a little. "Well, Madam, we're safely aboard."

Ella looked quickly around. She was overwhelmed by the grandeur she saw. Suspended from the ceiling was a huge chandelier with hundreds of sparkling crystal pendants. Here and there a potted palm stood beside the elaborately carved wood-paneled walls, a vivid splotch of green against the deep red plush carpeting. Endless rows of tables stretched out before her. Small shaded lamps shed a warm intimate light on the

snowy-white tablecloths. She was pleasantly aware of the sub-
dued hum of voices, the clinking of china, the silent movements
of the waiters as they served the fashionably dressed, important-
looking people. A bit apprehensive, she stayed close to Jules.

"There's a nice booth over there," Jules said, pointing.

The headwaiter hurried forward. "Two?" he asked politely.

"Two," Jules replied.

"This way, please."

With the feeling that all eyes were upon her, Ella followed
him through the maze of tables. It was hard to walk gracefully
in such narrow aisles.

At a small table off in a corner, the waiter halted, pulled
out a chair for Ella, and motioned grandly for them to be
seated. Jules half turned, looked at the booth, and cleared his
throat. "Er—do you mind—we'd rather have that booth,"
he said.

With a slight frown, the headwaiter resumed his march.

As she slid into the booth, Ella thought: Jules is a man
of the world; I wish I had his self-confidence.

She sat rigidly upright. Out of the corner of her eye, she
studied the couple at the next table. The man looked distin-
guished in his dark suit, with the tips of a white handkerchief

showing from his breast pocket, gold cuff links glinting from his sleeves. His companion wore a pearl-buttoned white linen suit and a large, floppy straw hat which framed her face. He was speaking in low tones, the woman listening attentively. Ella wondered if she could ever look as glamorous.

She watched with curiosity as the waiter placed before the couple something in a tall glass dish set in a bowl of ice. Casually the woman picked up one of several forks beside her and began to eat. I wonder what she's eating? I wouldn't even know which fork to use, Ella reflected wistfully. "It's so elegant here, Jules," she whispered.

"Yes," Jules replied matter-of-factly, "not bad." He twisted about impatiently. "Where is our waiter?"

A uniformed figure appeared at Jules's elbow. "Good evening," he said, placing two glasses of water before them.

Jules took a rapid glance at the menu. "What's special for today?" he asked.

"I'm sorry, sir," the man replied. "I'm the bus boy. You'll have to ask the waiter."

"Oh," Jules said, flushing a little.

A moment later a waiter was hovering over them, waiting to take their order.

What should I order, Ella wondered? There are at least

a hundred things to choose from. I don't even understand what these names mean. And what prices! Jules never should have picked such an expensive place.

Hurry up! Choose something fast! The waiter must be getting impatient. I bet he can tell I've never been in a place like this before.

She appealed to Jules. "What are you going to have?"

"Well—I don't know yet," he answered indecisively, pulling at his collar.

Desperately her eyes ran up and down the menu. Sandwiches! Why, of course! That was something easy to eat. You didn't have to cut it up or pick at it. You could eat a sandwich daintily, and it wouldn't cost so much, either. Lettuce and tomatoes—oh, no. That gets all sloppy and spilly. Egg salad, too. Sardines? Salmon? No—they'll make my hands smelly. Cheese! With relief, Ella spoke in a rush. "I'd like a cream cheese sandwich and a glass of milk, please."

"Cream cheese and milk!" Jules repeated. His eyebrows lifted in astonishment. "Is that all?"

"I'm not very hungry. I had a big dinner."

"Sure?"

"Sure."

"I'll have the same," Jules said, tossing the menu aside.

Bang! Bounce! Clatter! Jules dived under the table. He reappeared, red-faced, with a knife in his hand. "It's these big menu cards," he said, laughing a little. "Knocked it clean off the table." He handed the knife to the waiter. "Here, I'd like to trade this in for another one."

Ella marveled at his composure. If that had happened to me, she told herself, I would have died of shame. That comes from having so much experience, I guess.

She tried to think of a witty remark, but couldn't. Instead she picked up her glass of water and began to drink. Over the rim of her glass, she noticed that Jules also was drinking. Their eyes met. Quickly Ella turned away so that Jules couldn't see her gulping. They laughed uneasily as both their glasses came down at the same time. They kept looking in all directions, while the stillness between them grew more and more awkward. Jules strummed on the table with his fingers, and Ella prayed frantically for the waiter's return.

"Here comes our waiter now," Jules said brightly.

Ella gazed down at the cream cheese sandwich set before her. Beside it lay a luscious green olive. She loved olives, but better let this one go, she decided regretfully. She wasn't quite sure how one eats an olive in a restaurant. She picked up her sandwich, making sure to crook her little finger gracefully, and began to eat, taking small ladylike bites. She kept her eyes averted. Oh, dear, it's so embarrassing to eat when someone is watching you, especially when you want to make an impression.

"Aren't you going to eat your olive?" Jules asked. "I thought you liked olives."

"I do. But I just don't feel like olives right now."

They ate in silence. Ella noticed that Jules didn't touch his olive either. She was painfully conscious of the crawling slowness of each passing moment. Just as she was about to say something—anything—to fill the emptiness, Jules leaned forward and put his hand on hers. "You know, Ella," he said earnestly, "when two people go out to eat together for the first time, and they're uncomfortable, I think it's a sign that they think a lot of each other, don't you?"

Ella looked at him gratefully. This was one of the nice things about Jules—he was so understanding. "You were uncomfortable too?" she asked in disbelief.

"Was I?" Jules exclaimed. "From the very first moment we barged in here! And when that knife dropped, I wanted to sink through the floor! After all, I didn't know what to expect. This is the first time I've ever taken a girl to a restaurant!"

"Oh, Jules!" Ella sighed in great relief. "This is the very first time I've ever eaten in a restaurant!"

They looked into each other's eyes and all strain seemed to melt away. "Now, Ella," Jules said, grinning, "for a perfect evening, we ought to get up, go out, and come in again."

Abruptly Ella began to giggle. She felt lighthearted and gay.

The waiter appeared with his pencil and pad. "Begging your pardon, sir, but may I suggest as dessert our specialty, Parfait Royale?"

"Why, sure," Jules agreed with an easy wave of his hand, "bring us two of them."

In a few moments they were both gleefully digging into heavenly mounds of strawberry and vanilla frozen custard, marshmallow fudge, and whipped cream, topped with pink and white slices of nougat. Between mouthfuls, they chatted easily, as if they had been eating in restaurants together all their lives.

Out of the Frying Pan

At lunchtime the following Wednesday, Ella told her sisters: "I'll be going to the hospital this afternoon. But first I have to go to the library. Mama's finished her books and wants me to change them for her."

"Let's leave the dishes and wash them later," Henny proposed. "Then we can all go to the library."

"No," Ella replied quickly. "It's a long walk. Besides, someone has to stay around the house. Suppose Papa calls—or somebody else. Anyway, I have a date, and I don't want the whole family tagging along."

"Why didn't you say so in the first place, instead of beating around the bush," Henny said. "Isn't Jules working?"

"He is—that is, he was. Oh, I don't know . . ." Ella retreated into her room. That was bothering her, too. How could he get off in the middle of the day? Something must be up. When she asked him on the telephone last night, he wouldn't say. Just kept insisting he must see her today—that he had something very important to tell her.

She came back into the kitchen looking cool and summery in a fresh green and brown gingham dress. "My, how nice!" Charlotte exclaimed admiringly.

"Thank you. I feel nice, too."

"I wish we could see Mama," spoke up Sarah.

"So do I. Why don't they let young children in?" asked Gertie.

"Because they might bring sickness into the hospital," Ella explained.

"Now what'll we do with ourselves all afternoon?"

"You can come along with Charlie and me," Henny offered. "We're going to Crotona Park. We can watch the kids fishing for catfish in the lake."

"I'd like to," Sarah agreed.

"Gertie and I don't want to," Charlotte decided for both of them. "We'll stay home."

Ella picked up the library books and ran down the stairs.

At the landing, Grace was waiting for her with a bouquet of lovely dark Jack roses. "Here," she said, "these came out of our garden. Mother thought you'd like to take them with you."

"Oh, aren't they beautiful! Thank you, Grace! Mama'll be so pleased!"

The hall bell rang. "That's Jules," Ella cried, her cheeks growing pink. "I've got to go now. So long, Grace."

At sight of her, Jules's face lit up. "Hello, there," he said, relieving her of the flowers and the books. They walked together, her arm linked in his.

"Ella." Jules finally spoke. His voice sounded grave. "Ella," he repeated, "I've joined the Army."

The blood seemed to race away from Ella's heart. "But you couldn't! You're only nineteen. They're not drafting boys under twenty-one!"

"They take you at seventeen if you enlist."

"You haven't!"

"Yes, Ella, I already have."

"Why?" Ella was stunned. "What made you decide so suddenly?"

"It wasn't suddenly. I've been thinking about it ever since the war started. It wasn't easy to decide, Ella, believe me. But I had to do it. Can you see that?"

"It's not your duty—not till you're twenty-one!" Ella argued.

"Maybe not. It's hard to explain." He ran his fingers through his hair. "It's like this. Our parents, yours and mine, found the first real freedom they ever knew right here. By coming here, they made sure that their children would be free also. We can't let anyone take that freedom away, can we?"

Ella did not answer. Jules talked on earnestly. "We're Jews. You know tyrants have always tried to destroy us. In exactly the same way Germany is now trying to destroy little Belgium. Tyrants must be stopped—the sooner the better. That's why I can't sit around waiting till I'm twenty-one."

"I think I understand." Ella's voice trembled. "Only— when—when do you have to go?"

"Tomorrow."

"So soon?" She took hold of his hand and held it tightly.

By now they had reached the library. Jules paced up and down outside waiting for her. It did not take Ella long to exchange her books.

At the hospital door, Jules said, "I'd like to go in with you, Ella, but I can't stay too long. There are a million last-minute things to attend to, and I want to spend this last evening with my folks. You understand, don't you?"

They stood for a long time looking at each other. Jules tried to smile. "It's hard to say good-by."

Ella nodded, not trusting herself to speak. Tears welled up in her eyes. "Don't, Ella, please—" Jules pleaded. He bent down and kissed her on the cheek.

Meanwhile the two stay-at-homes were very busy stringing dried cantaloupe seeds on long white threads. "Mine don't lie straight," complained Gertie. "They go every which way."

"They're supposed to. You'll see, the necklace will look nice that way," Charlotte assured her.

Bz-zzz! Someone was pressing hard on the bell. "Who could that be?" Charlotte asked.

Dropping their necklaces, they hung over the banisters to see. "Why, it's Mrs. Shiner!" Charlotte whispered in surprise.

"Mrs. Shiner?"

"You know. The lady whose supper we ate. Don't you remember?"

By this time Mrs. Shiner had seen them. "Hello, darlings!" she called out. She came up, puffing, and hugging a package tight in one arm.

Shyly the girls led her into the parlor. Flopping down on the couch, Mrs. Shiner laid the package in her lap and let out a deep sigh. "Pfui, it's so steaming outside, everything sticks to you," she fretted, as she fanned herself vigorously with her purse. "Your Aunt Lena wrote me a letter from the country that your mama is sick in the hospital with an operation. I was so worried I had to come right over. So how is Mama now?"

"Oh, she's much better," Gertie answered.

"Thank God for that! Tell me, who's taking care of all you children while your mama is away?"

"We're taking care of ourselves," Charlotte replied proudly.

"All by yourselves! Can you imagine! Your mama is certainly lucky to have such smart children." She held out her package. "Here, darlings, I brought you something. So for one meal, anyhow, you shouldn't have to cook." She began to chuckle. "Now that I know already how much you like—you know what—I made sure to cook a big piece. Here, put it in the icebox."

"Corned beef! Oh, Mrs. Shiner, really you shouldn't!" Charlotte was overcome. "You're so kind—so thoughtful. Thank you so much!"

"Just wait till the others see this!" Gertie added gleefully.

"You're here all alone?" Mrs. Shiner asked, looking around.

"Uh-huh," Gertie answered. "Henny and Sarah and Charlie went to Crotona Park. And Ella's at the hospital."

"I'm sorry to miss them. Well, it can't be helped. Maybe I can go visit your mama at the hospital sometime."

"I think you have to have a pass for visiting, Mrs. Shiner, but you'll have to ask Ella about that," Charlotte said. "She'll be here round five o'clock. Couldn't you wait?"

"Well—" Mrs. Shiner's eyes surveyed the room again. "It's nice and cool here—and I got a little time—"

"We have some seltzer in the icebox. How about a cold drink?" suggested Charlotte.

"Oh, thanks. A cold drink I would certainly appreciate."

Gertie took her cue from Charlotte. "Please, not just seltzer, Mrs. Shiner. You have to have something to go with it. Mama always serves company something to eat."

Mrs. Shiner put up her hands to protest. "My dear children, don't bother yourselves. It's not necessary at all." Then suddenly she smiled at her two small hostesses and relaxed against the back of the couch. "All right," she said agreeably, "let me see what you can do."

Gertie ran and got Papa's newspaper. "Here, Mrs. Shiner, you can read while we're getting everything ready."

Mrs. Shiner was amused. "It's going to take so long?"

In the kitchen, the girls rushed about hunting through the icebox, the cupboard, the breadbox. "No cake and no crackers anywhere!" Charlotte said in dismay.

"What'll we give her?" Gertie worried.

"We ought to have something special that she'd really like. I know! A pancake!"

"A pancake!"

"Yes. A big pancake, like Mama makes!" Charlotte became inspired. "And we can serve it with strawberry jam!"

Gertie's eyes sparkled. This was going to be fun. Ella never let them do more than peel and wash vegetables and other boring things like that. Here was their chance to do some real cooking.

Soon the two little cooks were clothed in Mama's clean aprons. They ran around the kitchen collecting everything they needed. Charlotte took command. "You break open the eggs while I measure out the milk and flour."

Gertie smashed an egg against the mixing bowl. Cr-a-ck! The shell fell apart. The egg came slithering out on the table. In a panic she scooped up most of it and dumped it into the bowl. Her hands felt all gooey. She gazed at Charlotte ruefully. "Gee, eggs are awfully slippery. And it jumped out all of a sudden. You better open the next one."

Charlotte broke the second egg without mishap, then added a pinch of salt and some sugar. "Now Gertie," she ordered, "you pour in the flour gradually while I mix."

Charlotte began to beat vigorously with a wooden spoon. "It's so thick I can't pull the spoon around. Better start pouring in the milk, a little at a time."

The mushy lump began to thin out. It grew thinner and thinner until finally Charlotte yelled "Stop! That's way too much! Get more flour, quick!"

Flour and stir—flour and stir—at last the batter seemed right. Charlotte beamed with satisfaction.

"Why has it got all those lumps and bumps all of a sudden?" Gertie asked. "It never looks like this when Mama makes it."

Charlotte pondered. "I guess we didn't beat it enough." Again she beat and beat, till her arms ached, but the lumps just wouldn't go away.

"Now what'll we do?" Gertie asked in desperation.

Charlotte considered a moment. "I know. We'll strain it."

Slowly Charlotte pushed the doughy liquid through the wire mesh. It worked! The mixture came out smooth and creamy yellow. The girls heaved a sigh of relief.

Next Charlotte took out Mama's enormous frying pan. "Gee," she remarked, "this handle's kind of loose. It wobbles." She put a large pat of butter into the pan. When it sizzled, she poured in some batter.

They set the table while the pancake fried slowly and evenly on one side. Charlotte turned it over with great care. It was coming out just fine. A delicious buttery aroma spread through the room. "Mmm, mm!" Gertie sniffed appreciatively.

Mrs. Shiner came into the kitchen. "What smells so good?" she asked.

"It's a special kind of pancake we've made for you," Gertie said proudly. "It's ready now. Please sit down."

Mrs. Shiner waved her hands. "Oh, my, darlings! I didn't mean for you to go to all that trouble." But she sat down and waited to be served.

Charlotte viewed her creation with delight. It looked so appetizing. Its edges curled up crisply. Carefully she lifted the pan from the stove and carried it ever so slowly toward the table. Easy, now, she told herself, this handle is so wobb— with a suddenness that was startling, the handle turned in her grasp. The pan turned! Out slid the pancake! Kerplop—on

the floor! There it lay, a steaming circle of gold and brown, right at Mrs. Shiner's feet. And there was Charlotte, staring at the upside-down frying pan in her hand.

Gertie covered her eyes and shrieked. Mrs. Shiner clasped her hands in consternation. As for Charlotte, all she could say was, "Oh, oh! oh!"

Gertie dropped to her knees and with two fingers, daintily lifted the edge of the pancake. "It's still good, Mrs. Shiner," she said with a woebegone expression. "It's only been on the floor a little bit."

Charlotte looked down helplessly. "Aw, don't be silly."

But Gertie wouldn't give up. "Maybe we could wash it off," she said.

"Don't feel so bad, darlings," Mrs. Shiner said consolingly. "I'm sure the pancake would have tasted as good as it looked. I'll tell you what!" she added, with sudden inspiration. "Why don't we all go out for an ice-cream soda?"

At once the two gloomy cooks brightened. The unfortunate pancake was put in the garbage pail. Off came the aprons, and soon the girls were stepping joyfully alongside Mrs. Shiner on their way to the ice-cream parlor.

"I like tutti-frutti ice cream in my chocolate soda," Gertie told Mrs. Shiner happily.

A Good Week

Each morning, first thing, Charlie would ask, "Is Mama coming home today?" Each morning the answer was the same: "Not today, Charlie, but soon."

Every day now, there began to appear on their table what Charlotte called "the relative dish." On Monday Aunt Fanny showed up with a dish of homemade apple strudel. On Tuesday it was Aunt Olga with a dish of pickled herring. Wednesday brought Aunt Minnie with homemade noodles. And so on—all the hard-to-make things. Papa and the girls were very appreciative. It was good to have family in time of trouble.

The air was soft and balmy this Saturday evening as the children waited downstairs for Papa. Ella and Sarah sat gossiping on the low stoop. Charlie, with Henny holding onto him, teeter-tottered along the curb of the sidewalk. Gertie and Charlotte stood leaning over the stoop railing, peering through the window of Mr. Healy's butcher shop. "They sure are busy," Gertie said.

"Well, the Christians are shopping for their Sabbath," Ella told her.

"Our Sabbath is ending, and theirs is just beginning," observed Sarah.

"Ours isn't ending yet," Ella said, "Not till three stars appear in the heavens and Papa makes *Havdola*."

Sarah scanned the red-gold sky. "It takes a long time to get dark in the summer."

But in a little while the red-gold faded to gray, the street lights went on, and here was Papa back from evening services at the synagogue.

In the kitchen the children gathered around Papa for the *Havdola* ceremony. On the table lay a braided candle with many wicks, to resemble a torch when lit. Beside it stood the wine cup filled to overflowing—a symbol of hope that the coming week would be equally overflowing with good things. Here also was their beautiful, silver-ornamented spice box, pungent with the scent of the spices it contained. Just so would the fragrance of the Sabbath that was hastening away linger on throughout the entire week.

Charlie stood on tiptoe. This was his proud moment, as Papa allowed him to hold the lighted *Havdola* candle. He stood very still, gazing spellbound at the many-tongued flame.

First Papa chanted the blessing over the wine. Then, picking up the spice box, he shook it and set it down on the table again. He brought his hands close to the candle, his bunched fingers curving inward to make a shadow. Reverently the words fell upon the ears of the children:

"Blessed art Thou, O Lord our God, King of the Universe, who maketh us distinguish between light and darkness, between the seventh day and the six working days."

Now Papa poured a little of the wine on the table. Taking the candle from Charlie's grasp, he dipped it into the spilled wine. The flame sputtered—*Tzi-iszt!*—and died out. The Sabbath was ended. "A good week!" Papa proclaimed. "A good week!" the children cried in unison.

"Dip your fingers in the wine, Charlie, like we're doing," urged Gertie. "That's right. Now put them in your pockets. That means when we grow up we'll be very rich and always have lots of money in our pockets. Isn't that right, Papa?"

Papa grinned. "That's what my Papa told me. But there was something else he told me which is much more important," he went on. "The *Havdola* gives us the chance to worship God with all our five senses. Which one of you can explain that?"

Sarah spoke up. "Well, you *see* the light of the candle."

"You *hear* the prayer," added Charlotte, "and you *smell* the spices."

"You *taste* the wine," Gertie put in.

Henny began to count them off on her fingers. "Sight, sound, smell, taste—touch. That's what's missing—touch!"

"Right," said Papa. "And my fingers touch each other when I make the shadow."

"Papa, that's a beautiful way of thinking about the *Havdola*," Ella said.

"Yes, it is, agreed Papa. Happiness shone in his face. "The new week really has something good in store for us."

"What's that, Papa?"

"Mama's coming home tomorrow!"

"Oh, Papa!" "How wonderful!" The children began dancing and hugging one another for joy. Immediately they were full of plans. "We'll have to get up real early tomorrow and give the house a thorough going over," Ella said. "Everything must be in apple-pie order."

"Let's make a big WELCOME HOME sign and hang it over the front door," suggested Gertie.

"And make something special for supper that Mama likes," added Henny.

"We ought to get all dressed up like for a party," Charlotte joined in.

Charlie's feet wouldn't keep still. They went hippety-hop round and round the kitchen. "Mama's coming!" he sang over and over.

Sarah's eyes were shiny with tears. "I just can't wait!" she said.

It was more than an hour since Papa had left for the hospital. Dressed in their finest, the children were gathered around the stoop. Gertie and Charlotte, chafing with impatience, slipped off to the corner. They wanted to be the first to greet Mama.

"Too bad we haven't got a magic carpet handy," observed Henny. Just then Ella spotted Charlotte and Gertie bouncing up and down and waving frantically. "They're here!" she exclaimed. The children tore down the street like blurred streaks of lightning.

In a moment Mama found herself surrounded by her

family of laughing, jabbering youngsters. Papa's face beamed as he lifted his son high above the sea of skirts. Mama's arms reached out, and Charlie snuggled into them. "Mama! Mama!" he cried, hugging her tightly, as if he would never let her go.

They climbed up the stairs with everyone chattering away. Mama's eyes grew misty when she beheld the WELCOME HOME sign on the kitchen door. "I'm so happy," she murmured, and kissed them all.

Slowly she walked through the rooms, as if she were getting acquainted with everything all over again. "The house is spotless!" she declared with pleasure.

Ella noticed that Mama was looking pale. "Do you feel all right, Mama?" she asked.

Mama sank down on the edge of the bed. "I'm fine. Just a little tired."

Papa began shooing them out. "Come. Mama needs to rest now."

The Healys had been invited for supper. After the dishes were cleared away, everyone remained sitting around the table, nibbling at fruit and nuts. Mama took Mrs. Healy's hand. "Now at last I have a chance to thank you for all you've done."

"Go on, now. It was nothing," protested Mrs. Healy. "Nothing at all."

"Nothing!" Ella repeated. "Why, Mama, I don't know how we could have managed without Mrs. Healy and Grace. They were so helpful with meals and shopping and cleaning and everything."

"And don't forget Mr. Healy," Papa reminded.

"That's right," chuckled Mr. Healy, "mustn't forget him."

"Many times he took Charlie off my hands, Mama," Henny said. "He'd tell Charlie he needed him to help out. Charlie loved that."

"Yes, people have all been so wonderful," Mama said. "The doctor, the nurses, everyone. The relatives and many old friends from downtown came to visit me. So I spent most of the time chatting with them and knitting. I made two sweaters for the Red Cross and a nice warm pullover for Jules."

"Oh, Ma!" Ella exclaimed. "He'll be so pleased! He wrote me that August nights can get awfully chilly upstate where he's in training."

Later, Ella and Grace sat downstairs talking. "It's wonderful having Mama home again," Ella said. "I'm glad Mama had me to depend on, but you'll never know how worried I was all the time. Was I spending too much? Were we getting the right kind of meals? And the business of always having to tell someone what to do and when and how! And then afterwards wondering if it was the right thing to do in the first place! I tell you it was pretty frightening!" She took a deep breath. "Well, it's over now. I feel free as a bird!"

Henny joined them just in time to hear Grace answer, "Never mind, Ella, after this, taking care of only one husband will be a cinch!"

"Who wants to take care of a husband?" Henny put in scoffingly. "When I get married, my husband will take care of me!"

Ella smiled. Her fingers touched the letter she was carrying around in her jacket pocket. She had read it over and over many times since the postman brought it yesterday. She pulled it out and read parts of it again—" 'Well, they've given us our uniforms. They fit like a T. Only trouble is, who's got a shape like a T? . . . They have a well-balanced diet in this army. Every baked bean is exactly the same size as the next. . .'

"Listen to this, Grace. You'll be interested in this." Ella resumed her reading. " 'My buddy comes right from your neighborhood—just a few blocks from you. He's tall and blond and handsome—what you girls call the collar-ad type. He's a swell guy. No matter how tough the training gets, he's always ready with some funny remark which sets us all howling. Bill —his name is William Talbot—says he envies me the many wonderful letters I get from my girl. You know, Ella, even with hundreds of fellows around, a guy can get awfully lonely up here.

" 'I showed Bill your picture, and he thought you were mighty cute. But how could he possibly know how cute you really are? . . .' " Ella stopped reading. Some parts you just had to keep for your very own. She folded the letter and slipped it back into her pocket.

"That buddy certainly sounds like somebody I'd like to meet," Grace said.

"Soldiers do get a leave once in a while," answered Ella.

"You could write him and introduce yourself," Henny suggested.

"Oh, I couldn't do that!"

"Why not? I bet he'd love it. Everybody is always saying to write to the boys to keep up their spirits. I'm sure he'll answer. First thing you know, you'll be writing regularly."

"Oh—I don't know."

"Want me to write to Jules and ask him what he thinks?" Ella asked.

Henny brushed the idea aside. "Nah! Don't go dragging him into it. I'll tell you what. Everybody is knitting for the Red Cross—all kinds of things which are sent off to complete strangers. So why couldn't you send something you knit to Jules's friend. That's patriotic! What's wrong with being patriotic?

"Now—" Henny was getting wound up—"suppose you knit him a slipover like Mama made for Jules. Mama'll be glad to help you finish it in a hurry when you tell her it's for Jules's friend. Then you write a little note, and you pin it inside the sweater—and if you put in your picture too—that's that!"

Grace giggled. "Henny, you can think up the craziest schemes! But you know—I think I'll do it!"

P'Idyon Ha-Ben

Early one morning there was a banging on the kitchen door. "That could only be Uncle Hyman," Mama said. "He's the one that always bangs—Oh, my, do you suppose the baby has come? Come in," she called out.

The door opened, and Uncle Hyman swaggered in. "It's a boy!" he shouted. "My Lena's had a boy!" He danced around the room and snapped his suspenders. His small blue eyes and jolly round face were shining with happiness.

"Oh, Hyman, I'm so happy for you!" Mama cried, and the children gathered around, patting him on the back and dancing with him.

Papa grabbed Uncle Hyman by the shoulder. "A first

born and a son! That's really something to celebrate!"

"Yes!" declared Uncle Hyman. "My son will have the finest *P'Idyon Ha-Ben* a child could ever have! Everybody's invited—I mean everybody!" His eyes came to rest on Grace's astonished face. "And you too, young lady," he said, pointing at her. He dashed for the door. "I gotta go! I got a million things to attend to."

"Good-by, Hyman. Tell Lena we wish her all the best," Mama called after him.

Grace turned to Ella, "It's nice of your uncle to invite me, but what's he talking about?"

Ella laughed. "In Jewish families when the first child is a son, they have a ceremony which is called *P'Idyon Ha-Ben*. That means redemption of the son. It takes place one month after the child is born. It's a sort of party, really. You'll enjoy it."

A month seemed a long way off, but it was surprising how quickly the time passed. For days before, Mama had gone to Lena's house to help with the preparations. It was hard to tell who was more excited, Mama or Lena. "You'd think it was a *P'Idyon Ha-Ben* of her own," Papa teased.

When the family and Grace arrived on the party day, they found Lena's apartment already crowded with guests. Friends, neighbors, and relatives milled about in all their finery, glad to be together on such a joyous occasion.

Uncle Hyman and Aunt Lena were off in a corner, chatting with Mrs. Shiner. Catching sight of the family, all three pushed their way toward them. Lena, plumper and more rosy-cheeked than ever, kissed them heartily. "My beautiful nieces and my favorite nephew!"

"May we see the baby, Lena?" Gertie asked.

"Why not?"

They filed into the bedroom and tiptoed over to the crib. "Oh, how sweet!" "Isn't he cunning!" they whispered. "Look, Charlie, look at the tiny little baby."

Charlie stared at the infant. "It's like a doll."

The baby stirred and stretched his little arms over his head. His little face puckered. He yawned—a big, big yawn. "Yes, Charlie," Charlotte said, "it's a live doll!"

Uncle Hyman came in to remind them that it was time for the ceremony.

Charlie tugged at Mama's skirt. "Now can I see the pigeon?" he asked loudly.

They all stopped to listen to Charlie's strange request. "Pigeon," Mama repeated, puzzled. "What pigeon?"

Charlie explained patiently. "You said we were going to

a party and there's a pigeon and his name is Ben. I don' see no pigeon."

"Pigeon Ben! It does sound like it!" Henny squealed with laughter. "He means the *P'Idyon Ha-Ben*. He expected to see a real live pigeon!"

Why was everyone laughing so hard, wondered Charlie. "I wanna see Benny the pigeon!" he insisted.

Papa swept him up in his arms. "Charlie, what you're going to see is even better—like a little play. Come, and I'll explain it all to you while we're watching." He smiled at Grace. "And to you too, Grace."

In the parlor, the company had already arranged themselves in a wide circle. A tall, thin man dressed in a frock coat stepped forward. "That's the Cohan," Papa told Grace. "A Cohan is descended from the tribe of Aaron. Only such a one is allowed to perform this ceremony. In ancient times, the oldest son was required to serve in the Temple. If one wanted to release his child from this service, he had to pay for it. Today the Cohan will act like the High Priest in the Temple of old."

The room grew quiet. Presently Uncle Hyman appeared from the bedroom. On a cushion in his arms lay the baby, dressed in an exquisitely embroidered white dress. Solemnly he walked to the Cohan and offered the child up to him. He began

to recite in Hebrew. Grace turned to Papa inquiringly. In a
low whisper, Papa translated. "This, my first born, is the first
born of his mother . . ."

The Cohan took the child from his father. "Which do you
prefer," he asked, "to give me thy first born for God's service
. . . or to redeem him for five shekels which you are by law
required to give?"

Charlie pulled on Papa's hand. "Papa, why is that man
taking the baby from Uncle Hyman?"

"Don't worry, Charlie. Uncle Hyman'll get him back."

Uncle Hyman held up five silver dollars and answered the Cohan. "I prefer to redeem my son. Here is the value . . . which I am by law obliged to pay."

The Cohan accepted the money and returned the child to Uncle Hyman. Holding the coins over the infant's head, the Cohan proclaimed: "*This* is an exchange of *that*. . . . May it be the will of God that . . . this child may be spared to enter the study of the law, the state of marriage, and the practice of good deeds. Amen!"

Placing his hands upon the baby's head, he blessed the little one: "The Lord shall guard thee against all evil . . . Amen!"

"Amen!" answered the guests. "May you have much joy and honor from him!" They crowded around, ohing and ahing over the baby and showering congratulations on the parents.

As the guests circled about, Uncle Hyman started shooing them toward the dining room. "Let's go to the table! Let's go to the table!" he coaxed.

They didn't need much urging. The sight of the table piled high with delicious-looking food whetted everyone's appetite. Uncle Hyman scurried around filling glasses with schnapps or wine.

Everyone ate heartily—laughing and singing and telling stories in between. They complimented Lena on her excellent cooking, and her rosy face blushed even rosier with pleasure. Everybody was having a fine time.

It was late when at last the party began to break up. Tired and happy, the family groups started to leave. "May we always come together on joyous occasions," was the parting wish as they fondly embraced one another.

"Girls," Lena whispered as she put her arms around Ella and Grace, "being married and having a baby is the most wonderful thing in the world. *Merchum* by you!" (May it happen to you.) For answer, Ella kissed Aunt Lena.

"Thank you so much for letting me come," Grace said. "I really enjoyed it."

"I'm glad," Uncle Hyman beamed. "Come again. Any time you like."

Charlie was so tired that Papa had to carry him all the way home. They were just entering the house when the little boy suddenly raised his head. "Papa," he asked, "does the Cohan keep all the pigeon money for himself?"

"Oh, no, Charlie," replied Papa. "The *P'Idyon Ha-Ben* money goes to charity."

Round and Round

In a wall in Mama's kitchen was a small door which opened onto the dumb-waiter shaft. The dumb-waiter was a large wooden cabinet attached to a pulley rope. It could be hauled up and down like an elevator. When the family first moved uptown, it was the dumb-waiter which fascinated the children most. "Dumb-waiter!" Gertie giggled. "Do they mean it's stupid?"

Actually it was a handy silent servant. Tradespeople found it especially useful. For instance, the seltzer man, instead of trudging up long flights of stairs with a heavy case of bottles, put it on the dumb-waiter and hoisted it up. It saved Mr. Healy steps too. Every morning Mama would send the garbage pail down to the basement. Mr. Healy would empty it and send it back up to Mama.

It was Charlie, though, who enjoyed the dumb-waiter the most. The cabinet was exactly the right size for a small boy. Charlie would crawl into it and have his sisters pull him up and down.

Also the two families could get in touch with one another quickly through the dumb-waiter shaft. One morning when Ella answered the dumb-waiter buzzer, she could see Grace's red head turned up toward her. "Ella, guess what?" Grace held up a white envelope. "It came!"

"From Jules's buddy?"

"Uh-huh. He sent his picture. He's so good-looking!"

"What does he say?"

"He wants to see me next Sunday to thank me for the slip-over. He's getting a week's leave. Come on down, and I'll show you the letter."

Ella tried hard to share Grace's enthusiasm when she read the letter, but she was worried. Jules was also getting leave. He hadn't said a word, but Ella knew that such a leave could mean only one thing—they were being shipped overseas. It was terrible, liking somebody an awful lot and then having him go away—and you could not see him again for heaven knows how long! To be wondering all the time he was away—was he all right, would he ever come back? In a panic, she thrust the dreadful thoughts out of her mind. Think only about now! Think about the glorious week when Jules will be here! She forced herself to smile as she said, "You write Bill and tell him Sunday will be fine. He can come over with Jules."

"Oh, Ella, you didn't tell me Jules was getting leave too! Isn't that marvelous!"

It was the day! Any minute now Jules would arrive with his friend. Ella and Grace kept circling around the parlor, wondering where to sit or where to stand to make the prettiest picture when the boys first saw them.

"Henny, please get away from the window," Ella begged. "It makes such an awful impression."

"Yes, Henny, please," Grace added her plea. "It makes us seem anxious."

"Well, aren't you?"

"But we don't have to show it!" Grace replied. "Boys get awfully conceited if you make a fuss over them."

"Hey, there they are!" Henny leaned way out, waving her hand excitedly and yelling at the top of her lungs, "Hi there, soldiers!"

"Henny!" Ella and Grace cried out, horrified.

Henny went scooting into the bedroom where Sarah sat at her desk studying history. "Sarah, the soldiers are here!"

"Yes," Sarah replied vaguely, absorbed in her history lesson.

"Oh, Sarah, will you forget about that history prize for once? Didn't you hear me? I said the soldiers are here! Come on!"

Sarah jumped up. "Oh, Jules and Bill!" In a moment she and Henny were back in the parlor.

Ella stamped her foot. "Both of you, will you please leave at once, and for heaven's sake, keep out of the parlor—for a little while, at least! If the whole family falls on top of Grace's visitor, he'll be so embarrassed he'll want to run!"

"Okay! Okay!" Henny and Sarah retreated to the kitchen.

Ella stood expectantly at the open parlor door. In a few minutes Jules's dear, familiar voice was crying out her name. "Ella!" A pair of strong arms enfolded her in a quick hug.

Ella could not take her eyes off him. How handsome he was! Slim and wonderfully fit! "Jules, you look just grand in uniform!" she said.

Behind them, a surprisingly deep but gentle voice asked, "How about me? Don't I look grand in my uniform?"

Ella and Jules whirled about. They'd almost forgotten about Bill! Full of apologies, Jules introduced his friend. My, but he's big, thought Ella—a blond giant! He must be over six feet! Lucky thing Grace isn't a shrimp like me.

Bill took her hand; it was so small in his. "You're a little bit of a thing," he said, with a grin.

"All good things come in small packages, you know," Jules answered.

Ella smiled. Bill was nice. She liked his strong, broad face,

the cleft in his chin, the laughing gray eyes. "Come and meet Grace," she said, leading him into the parlor.

"So this is the kind lady who took pity on a poor lonely soldier," Bill said, sliding down on the couch beside Grace. "Hello, Grace. Thanks so much for the letters as well as the slipover." He chuckled and cocked his head to one side. "You're even prettier than your picture."

Grace blushed, but Ella could tell that she was pleased. It was going to be fun—the four of them together.

Alas, her bliss did not last long. Scarcely had they begun to talk when the whole family came swarming into the parlor. "Hello, Jules!" "How are you?" "How do you like army life?" "Gee, you look wonderful! Turn around so we can see the back!"

In the midst of the hubbub, Ella attempted to introduce Bill to the various members of the family. He's bound to feel awfully uncomfortable with all this mob, she worried. But Bill seemed to be enjoying himself enormously. "I see you've got your own army," he remarked to Papa, and that set everyone laughing.

Charlie planted himself in front of the stranger. Hands behind his back, he looked him up and down very carefully. "Where's your gun?" he demanded.

Bill tousled the boy's hair. "I left it back in camp."

"How can you fight with no gun?"

"Oh, I can fight all right. Want to see?" Playfully he poked Charlie in the ribs. "Bang! Bang! Bang! You're dead!"

Charlie tumbled to the floor. But in a moment he was on his feet to do battle again.

"Say, I thought you were dead!" Bill said.

"Now I'm another guy," Charlie answered promptly.

"Oh, excuse me! I got you mixed up with that other feller. How do you do?" They shook hands gravely. "Let's be friends and not fight any more. Okay?"

"Okay," agreed Charlie, and he stood by Bill's side gazing up at him admiringly.

"It's a lot of fun belonging to a big family," Bill said to Mama. "At least I always thought so, being an only child myself."

"It must have been lonely for you," Mama replied in quick sympathy.

Bill grinned. "No, not really. I was quite a handful all by myself."

Jules turned to Mama. "That sweater you made me sure comes in handy on these cold nights. I haven't had a chance to thank you yet."

Mama beamed at him. "I'm glad you like it, Jules."

"How about you, Bill? Anybody ever knit anything for you?" Henny asked, with a knowing wink at Grace.

Bill's eyes met Grace's. "Yes. Somebody did. A fine slipover, just like Jules's. I'll be nice and warm this winter too."

Ella squeezed Grace's arm. Grace took the hint. "Well, Bill, Jules, Ella, how about coming down to my house?"

The week that followed was a glorious one for the four friends. "I wish it would never end!" Grace exclaimed.

How her eyes shine! Ella thought. Her whole face seems to glow. She smiled at Grace. "I know. I feel as if I'd like to hug every day close to me."

But there was no holding back the time. All too soon, it was Sunday evening. "Our last night together," Jules said soberly.

They took the streetcar which crossed to Manhattan. Here they could board a double-decker bus. "Let's wait for the one that'll give us the longest ride. Might as well get our money's worth," Bill said, laughing.

At this hour the bus was nearly empty. "It's mighty blowy upstairs today," the conductor warned politely as they climbed aboard.

Bill puffed out his chest. "After our army training, we're regular Eskimos."

The bus lurched forward. Everyone held on for dear life, laughing boisterously. Clinging to the hand rail, they climbed up the steep spiral staircase to the upper deck. The bus pitched and rolled like a ship as they went stumbling down the aisle and tumbled into the front seats.

The conductor held out his shiny coin machine. "Ooh, let me put the dimes in," Ella begged like a little girl. Each time a coin was pushed into the narrow slot a bell tinkled, and Ella giggled as she felt the dime being sucked from her fingers.

The bus turned into Riverside Drive. Autumn had touched the trees, turning their leaves to brown and gold. Beyond the grassy slope lay the flat Hudson River, the electric signs on the Jersey shore glinting on its slate-blue water. Before them the expanse of twilight sky stretched wide. The wind whistled past their ears, caught hold of every loose strand of hair. The couples snuggled cosily on the benches just big enough for two.

For a while they rode in silence. To Ella the bus wheels seemed to be revolving in a mournful chant—"the last time together—the last time—the last time—the last time . . ." Was it the wind which made her feel so cold suddenly, she wondered? She shivered. Jules's arm tightened around her shoulder.

I mustn't spoil the last evening. It has to be a happy time to remember afterward. I mustn't think about tomorrow— just about now! She began to hum softly. "Let's sing something together," suggested Jules. So Ella let her voice come out full and strong. "Oh, how lovely is the evening—is the evening . . ." and Jules joined in on the next line.

"That's great!" declared Bill. "Let's try it again, and Grace and I'll sing too."

Ella started over. On the second line a clear, high tenor voice chimed in. It was the conductor! He was standing on the top step with one hand holding on to the rail, the other on his chest like an opera singer, his head tilted back.

As the round ended, the buzzer sounded. The bus slowed down. "I'll be right back!" the conductor shouted, starting down the stairs. When the bus started up again, he reappeared. "Had to collect a coupla fares," he apologized. "How about 'Row, row, row your boat'?" Beating time with his arm, he sang the first line, and the two couples joined in.

Again the buzzer sounded. The conductor shook his head sadly and disappeared down the steps. He was back in a jiffy. "Say, folks," he pleaded, "why don't you come downstairs? Then we won't get interrupted. My pal, the driver, has a bass voice, real deep, like a foghorn. And he's anxious to get in on this."

"But what about the passengers," Grace asked. "Won't they mind?"

The conductor chuckled. "Don't worry. There'll be no extra charge for the entertainment. They'll enjoy it."

"Come on, let's go!" said Bill. "This should be a lot of fun."

They scrambled out of their seats and went below. Downstairs the bus was quite full. "Excuse me, lady," the conductor said to a woman sitting up front, "would you mind changing your seat? These are the singers, an' they gotta sit close together, you know."

Puzzled but obliging, the woman moved to the rear, and the four young people settled themselves on the seats behind the driver. The conductor held up his hand. "Passengers, attention!" he announced. "You will now have the pleasure of hearing for the first time, the Fifth Avenue Bus Singing Society!"

Immediately the singers swung into "There's a long, long trail a-winding into the land of my dreams." When the song was ended, the astonished passengers applauded enthusiastically. Someone called out "More!" Someone else yelled, "How about that new song—you know— 'Over There!'"

The conductor rapped for silence and the Singing Society started. "Johnny get your gun, get your gun, get your gun. Take it on the run, on the run, on the run." The passengers began swaying with the catchy tune. Soon several joined in, and by the time they had reached the chorus, everybody was singing.

The bus had turned away from the Drive and was now rolling down Fifth Avenue. Past stately mansions and old churches—past the library where the twin lion statues stared placidly—past the magnificent shops with their beautiful displays.

All at once a lady passenger jumped up with a loud cry. "Oh, my goodness! It's Fourteenth Street already! I got so interested in the singing, I forgot to get off at Thirty-fourth Street. Now what'll I do?"

"Take it easy, lady," the conductor told her. "We'll be headin' back uptown. So sit down and enjoy yourself. We've just about enough time for another round." He started them off. "Are you sleeping, are you sleeping?" One after another the singers took up the round. "Brother John, Brother John." "Morning bells are ringing, morning bells are ringing," boomed the driver. "Ding! Dong! Ding!" clanged the warning bell beneath his foot. "Ding! Dong! Ding!" the conductor answered, yanking the bell cord.

All too soon, Washington Arch hove into sight. The bus rushed toward the last stop . . .

They were home. Now was the time for saying good-by. All week long they had dreaded this moment. All week long they had covered up their feelings with gaiety and laughter. Now it was no longer possible to hide the fear and loneliness of parting.

Ella raised misty eyes to Jules. He cleared his throat. "You must write, Ella. Every day! Every single day!"

Ella nodded. She leaned her head on Jules's shoulder.

Bill's fingers entwined themselves in Grace's. He looked down at her sad face. "Good-by, dearest Grace," he whispered.

For a while no one spoke. Then Jules said, "We've got to go."

Ella tried forlornly to smile. She made her voice sound very bright. "All right! One last song, everybody! 'When you come back, and you will come back—' " she began bravely, and the others joined in.

The song was finished. Bill and Jules saluted stiffly. They turned on their heels and marched swiftly down the street. Tears rolling down their cheeks, the girls stared silently after them until they were gone from sight.

The Naughty Nickel

"Tanta Olga could use one of you girls this afternoon," Mama said at breakfast.

Tanta Olga was a seamstress. She made the most beautiful men's silk shirts. Sometimes she got so busy she couldn't keep up with her orders. Not having any daughters of her own, she'd call on Mama's girls for help. Just to do the small things, like sewing on buttons or snipping basting threads.

"I'll go," Charlotte spoke up quickly. Charlotte liked to sew. She once explained to Gertie, "You can think about things and make up the most interesting stories while you're sewing." Besides, Tanta Olga always gave her ten cents for the afternoon's work.

"I've been saving up," she said. "With the ten cents I'll make today, I'll be able to buy another twenty-five cent thrift stamp to paste on my card."

"Now President Wilson will surely be able to buy everything we need for the war," teased Henny.

"Never you mind, Henny," Sarah retorted. "Miss Brady says it may seem like a little, but Charlotte's stamps, and yours, and mine, and everyone else's all over the country, add up to a lot of money."

"And don't forget," Ella went on, "you get interest on your money."

"But you have to wait five years before you can collect," Henny reminded her.

"I can wait," Sarah replied evenly. "Especially when it means I'm lending my money to my country."

"I like the little sayings they have in the spaces where you paste the stamps," Gertie remarked. "Which one are you up to, Charlotte?"

Charlotte ran to get her thrift card. "Number nine," she announced. "It says, 'Many a little, makes a mickle.' "

Charlie was attracted by the sound of the words. "Many a mickle . . . nickel makes a nickel mickle." He giggled as his tongue got all twisted up.

"I'm way ahead of you," Sarah cried. "I'm up to this one —'Great oaks from little acorns grow.' Just one more and I'll have the whole card filled. I wish I could go with you, Charlotte, but I've got to stay home and study my history. I have to keep on getting the highest marks if I want to win the prize."

"If you keep on the way you've been doing, you ought to have a pretty good chance," Ella said reassuringly.

"I know, but that Dorothy Miller's awfully smart. She's the only one in my class I'm really worried about."

"Remember, Sarah," Mama said quietly, "work should be done for its own sake, not just for a prize."

"I know, Mama, but still it would be so wonderful to win the prize."

On her way to the El, Charlotte hugged her library book to her. It was such a thrilling story—so strange and mysterious. It gave her goose-pimples all over! All through school, she could hardly wait to get on with it. Thumbing eagerly through the pages, she found her place and started to read. She walked slower and slower, completely caught up in the story. This was not the Bronx; she was not on her way to Tanta Olga's. She was in far-off England, on a lonely heath with the wind howling eerily about her.

"Hello, there! What are you reading that's so absorbing?" a voice spoke above her. Charlotte didn't even hear. A hand touched her shoulder. Charlotte's head came up, her dreamy blue eyes blinked at Miss Brady.

"You really shouldn't be reading while walking," Miss Brady admonished gently. "It's bad for your eyes." She turned the book over in Charlotte's hand. *Wuthering Heights.* She smiled in understanding. "I can hardly blame you. That's one book anybody would find hard to put down. Still, you must be careful. You might bump into something."

"I know," Charlotte nodded seriously, "but I just couldn't wait to find out what happens."

Miss Brady beamed at her. "I'll be looking forward to having such a good reader in my history class next year." She held up a small paper bag and shook it. It gave a sharp, rattling sound. "I'm collecting prune pits. Did you have prunes for breakfast this morning?" she asked with a twinkle in her eye.

Charlotte stared at her. "Why—er—no," she said, non-plused.

"Will you be having them tomorrow?"

"I don't know. I guess so—maybe."

Miss Brady wagged a playful finger at her. "From now on, we must save all the pits from prunes, apricots, and peaches, and deposit them in a special red, white, and blue can you'll find on the street corner. This is something new which our government has asked us to do."

"Why should we do that?" Charlotte asked, open-mouthed.

"They'll be burnt into charcoal, and then the government will use the charcoal to put into gas masks. You'll be hearing all about it in assembly tomorrow morning."

By now they were at the station. From a distance, Charlotte could hear the clackety-clack of an oncoming train. Oh, dear! She didn't want to miss that train. Tanta Olga always liked her to come early. "Good-by, Miss Brady," she cried hastily, and went bounding up the long staircase to the elevated platform high above the street.

She had almost reached the platform when the train pulled in. Already people were streaming through the opened exit gate at the head of the stairs. "Excuse me!" she gasped as she elbowed her way through and went sprinting madly down the platform. The very instant she hopped aboard, the conductor slammed the door shut. She laughed aloud in triumph. She'd made it! With a sudden violent jerk, the train moved away from the station and Charlotte, all breathless, hurtled into the nearest seat.

She sat still for a minute, recovering her breath. She sighed blissfully. Now she could return to her *Wuthering Heights*. But first she had to blow her nose. She pulled her handkerchief out of her pocket. It had a hard lump in one corner where a knot had been tied. Inside was her money. Money! "Ooh!" It suddenly came to her. I forgot to pay my carfare! Gee willikers! That's awful.

She was puzzled. How did it happen? She tried to remember. When you got to the station, you were supposed to go to the booth and buy a blue paper ticket for a nickel. Then you took it over to the ticket chopper. The ticket chopper man always stood behind the tall wooden box, the top chamber of which was made up of two sides of wood and two of glass. Through one side ran a sharp cleaver attached to a handle on the outside of the box. When you dropped in your ticket, the ticket chopper man let you pass. When the chamber was quite full of tickets, he worked the handle up and down, and all the tickets would get chopped up into little bitsy pieces. Then they'd drop down into the bottom of the box where you couldn't see them any more.

But she hadn't even stopped to buy a ticket! She had just rushed through the exit gate and boarded the train in the nick of time. Warily she looked around at the other passengers.

Did they know what she'd done?

She squeezed the handkerchief knot. A whole nickel! A person could get an awful lot for a nickel! For instance, a pad— a really, truly good one like the Square Deal kind which had such smooth, white paper. I could write my homework on it beautifully with ink. Or one of those tiny pink celluloid dolls from the Five and Ten. I'd have such fun dressing it for Gertie. I could get a Napoleon! It melts in your mouth with creamy custard just oozing out all over! Or even five Indian Bars with nuts inside! Then I'd give two to Gertie and keep three for myself! Mmm . . . mmmm. Charlotte smacked her lips.

With all that crush at the gate, I bet nobody even noticed. Otherwise, wouldn't the ticket seller have yelled after me? So what am I worrying about? For once I got a free ride and now I have a nickel all for myself!

It's not yours! A voice inside her spoke up so loudly, she wondered if anyone else had heard.

I don't care! she answered herself defiantly. With all the nickels the train company has, what difference does one little nickel make? They wouldn't even miss it.

That still doesn't make it right, the voice promptly replied. It's stealing!

Charlotte squirmed uneasily. She began to plead with herself. If I add it to my other savings and buy war stamps with it, wouldn't that make it all right?

She shook her head. No. You can't fix it up that way. The Government wouldn't want a cheated nickel! She pushed the handkerchief out of sight into her coat pocket.

Clackety clack—clackety clack

Give it back—give it back!

the train wheels rattled warningly.

No! It was hers! All hers! She opened her book and tried to read. But it was no use. The nickel seemed to be dancing on the page before her. She reached her station and got off. Somehow she had the feeling that the naughty nickel had stood up on its narrow rim and was rolling along behind her all the way to Tanta Olga's.

All afternoon as Charlotte painstakingly stitched pearl buttons to the delicate silk shirts, Tanta Olga noticed that she was even quieter than usual. Finally, at half past five, Tanta Olga said, "That's enough for today, Charlotte. I must say, you certainly didn't waste a minute. Here is a dime for you and another one for the fares." Charlotte drew on her coat and fled from the house before her astonished aunt could even say good-by.

At her home station, Charlotte trotted down the long flight of stairs to the street below. All she needed now was to round the corner and walk two blocks to home. Instead she crossed the street to the uptown side and marched steadily up the stairs straight to the ticket seller's window.

"Please, Mr. Ticket Man," Charlotte's voice pleaded, "take back the nickel."

The ticket seller looked at her quizzically. "Why, young lady? Isn't it a good one?"

"No! It's been following me around all afternoon!"

The man's eyebrows shot up. He leaned forward. "That's very interesting. Tell me all about it."

Slowly the story came out. "So here's the nickel back," Charlotte finished.

The man nodded gravely. Tearing a ticket from his big round roll, he pushed it through the opening. "Drop the ticket into the chopper, young lady, and then come back here," he ordered.

Charlotte did as she was told. But she was worried. Why did he want her to come back?

A trembling Charlotte stood before the ticket seller once more. She raised her eyes. Why, he wasn't scowling or angry at all. He was smiling. "I've got something for you," he said. He took something out of his pocket and held it up for her to see. "It's a *good* nickel! A present for you," he said, shoving it through the window. "Because you're such an honest girl."

They looked at each other and grinned.

The Red Boogey Man

The weeks rolled by, and the time arrived for the Jewish High Holy Days. The day before Rosh Hashana Miss Brady said to the class, "Children, tomorrow a new year begins for the people of the Jewish faith. All of us know that now it is 1917, but who can tell us the date of the coming Jewish year?"

Only Sarah raised her hand. "5678," she declared proudly.

"That's right," said Miss Brady, with an approving nod.

Yom Kippur, the Day of Atonement, came and went, and finally it was Succos, the Harvest Festival. For the first time Papa was not building his own Succah, and the family felt a little sad. Mr. Healy would have been glad to allow Papa the use of his back garden for the little wooden hut, but Papa said no. He explained to the children that the members of the neighborhood synagogue were building a big Succah where all would celebrate together.

For a long time there had been no word from either Jules or Bill. And then the letters started coming. They were somewhere in France in the thick of the fighting. The letters were chatty and cheerful, but Grace and Ella worried.

Along came December and Hanukkah, the Festival of Lights. One night Grace was watching Ella fix a package to be sent to Jules overseas. "My, that's an awful lot of sweets you're sending!" she exclaimed.

"To give him a lot of sweet thoughts about me," Ella said wistfully.

Henny snorted. "If it doesn't give him indigestion first!"

When Ella had finished, Grace said, "Now how about coming down and helping me get Bill's box ready?"

Ella was humming a catchy little tune as they went down the stairs. "What's that you're singing?" Grace asked.

"It's a Hanukkah song." Ella translated:

> Oh ye little candle lights!
> Ye tell us tales without end.
> Ye tell of battle, heroism, and glory
> Wonders of long ago!

"You know," Grace mused, "it's odd how much your

Hanukkah is like our Christmas. The candles, singing of special holiday songs, and the children getting presents . . ."

"Yes," agreed Ella, "there are many things that are alike about our holidays. For instance, eggs are important in your celebration of Easter. Well, eggs play a big part in our Seder service at Passover. Then you have Lent when you fast and deny yourselves the eating of certain foods. During Passover week, we also deny ourselves eating of bread and other year-round foods. There are lots of other similar things like that."

"That's so," Grace said thoughtfully, as she opened her kitchen door. "I guess all religions have many things in common. Not just holidays, either."

"Speaking of holidays, Grace," Mrs. Healy observed, "we haven't half finished all the things we have to do. And Christmas practically upon us."

"It'll be a sad Christmas for many a family this year," Mr. Healy said soberly.

"And especially sad for Bill's folks," Mrs. Healy added. "After all, he's their whole family."

"Maybe we ought to invite them over to help us trim the tree," suggested Mr. Healy.

"That would have been nice," Grace said, "but they won't be here. They're spending Christmas with relatives."

"How do you trim a tree?" Ella asked.

"You mean to say you've never seen one?" Grace cried.

"Only in pictures," replied Ella. "Where we lived on the East Side, it was all Jewish and there weren't any."

"For goodness sake!" Grace marveled. "Well, you'll see one this year for sure."

"That is," Mrs. Healy interposed, "if it is all right with your folks."

That very night Mrs. Healy spoke to Papa. He deliberated a moment, then answered. "So long as it's just to look, that would be all right."

So it was that on Christmas Eve, Mama's children came downstairs to visit with the Healys. The parlor door was opened wide, but on the threshold, no one moved. The children stood awestruck.

The room was almost dark except for one corner where a graceful little fir tree stood. Many candles gleamed on its green branches, and glittering ornaments added bright spots of color. "Oh! It's like a fairyland!" Charlotte murmured.

Gertie breathed the fresh, woodsy smell. "Ah-h. It has such a wonderful fragrance!"

The gleaming ornaments beckoned invitingly to Charlie. They were so shimmery, all different shapes and sizes! What did they feel like, he wondered? Some of the tinselly things dangled on the low branches, tantalizingly near. All he had to do was stretch out his hand . . .

"Careful, Charlie!" Ella cried out.

But Charlie was too entranced to heed. Lovingly, with gentle fingers, he caressed a shiny globe. Why, it was so light it felt like nothing! He let go, and the branch bounced back. The bright ball shook off and fell. With a soft, splintery sound, it shattered. Charlie stared at the bits of glass. It was all broken!

"Oh, Charlie!" scolded Ella, "you were told to be careful!"

"Sure, don't you worry about it, Ella," Mrs. Healy said. "Let him enjoy it. It's not the first one broken today, nor will it be the last."

All at once, from the hallway, there came the jingle, jangle of many bells. Grace held up a finger. "Listen, Charlie," she said, "do you hear?"

Louder and nearer the bells sounded till the air was filled with their ringing. "Whoa, Donner and Blitzen!" a rollicking voice roared. Now someone was knocking on the parlor door. "Ho! Ho! Ho! Open up and let me in!"

The door flew back, and there stood a roly-poly, jolly old man with a long, flowing white beard. He was dressed all in bright red, even to the tasseled cap on his snowy white head.

Face rosy with laughter and eyes all a-twinkle, he came stamping into the parlor. "Ho! Ho! Ho!" he bellowed again, and he patted his big, fat tummy.

Charlie gazed at him fascinated. Never had he seen anybody like this before. He was big as a mountain! And such a thundering voice!

"Aha! Here's a nice little feller. Have you been a good

boy?" The giant was growling at him now. He was coming
nearer. Charlie began backing away. Something about him
seemed familiar. Like a flash, he knew who it was—this was
the boogey man! The terrible boogey man who lurked in dark
corners always ready to spring out at you if you had been a bad
boy. The boogey man had come to catch him, to take him away
from Mama and Papa, and everybody. "Go away, boogey
man!" he screamed. "You bad, bad boogey man!"

Everyone burst into laughter. "No, no, Charlie, that's not
a boogey man," Grace tried to explain. "That's Santa Claus."

But Charlie didn't wait. He bolted out of the room and
up the stairs as fast as his little legs could carry him, calling,
"Mama! Mama! Mama!"

"Oh, my!" Mrs. Healy was flabbergasted. "He really was
frightened."

"Don't be too upset, Mrs. Healy. After all, he's never even
heard of Santa Claus," Ella said, smiling.

Santa plucked off his whiskers, revealing a perspiring Mr.
Healy. "I thought I was going to give the youngsters a bit of
fun," he remarked ruefully. "Instead I wind up scaring the
wits out of the little feller. Do I look as bad as all that?"

Grace laughed. "Not at all, Dad. I think you look grand.
You see," she went on, "Dad's going to play Santa Claus at a

children's party at the hospital tomorrow, and he just couldn't wait to try out his costume on us."

"I'd better go up and tell Mama what happened," Ella said, as she started for the door. "She'll be wondering what it's all about. C'mon, kids, let's all go. Thanks very much for letting us see your tree, Mrs. Healy. It's really very beautiful."

Several days later Ella came down to the Healy household to show Grace her latest letter from Jules. It was then that Grace remarked, "It's more than a month since Bill's last letter. I can't understand it."

"Well, you know how uncertain mail is during wartime," Mrs. Healy said, reassuringly.

The phone rang. "It's for you, Grace," Mr. Healy called out. "It's Mrs. Talbot."

"Bill's mother?" Grace cried. "Maybe she's gotten word from Bill." She flew to the phone. "Hello! Yes, this is Grace."

The others sat quietly watching, but even as they watched, Grace's face grew pale. They could see her hand on the receiver tightening till the knuckles showed white. A sudden fear touched everyone.

"Oh, no!" Grace was whispering into the phone. Helplessly she turned to her mother, the phone dropping from her grasp.

Mrs. Healy grabbed hold of the receiver. "Hello! This is Mrs. Healy. What is it? What's happened?" she cried. "Yes, yes, yes . . . I see. Oh, how dreadful!" She put her hand over the mouthpiece and spoke to Mr. Healy. "It's Bill—there was a telegram—he's missing in action."

Grace sat down, looking dazed. "Oh, Bill!" she sobbed.

Ella looked at her friend dumbly.

No one could think of anything to say.

Play for Shavuos

The newspapers were reporting fierce fighting on the battle-fields of France. Wherever one looked there was a poster telling everybody to save for victory. "Buy War Stamps! Keep on Buying!"

"Uncle Sam needs that extra shovelful of coal!" cautioned a sign near the elevated. Since early in January, every Monday was a Heatless Day. On that day, all factories except those working for the war shut down.

Over the entrance to Papa's cellar a sign read, "Your country needs your junk. Sell to any peddler." Every bit of scrap iron, even tin cans, went into peddlers' sacks.

But it was food saving that was most important. Lessons

were given in cooking without waste. People were urged to do without sugar, meat, fat, flour, so that these might be shipped to the soldiers and to our starving allies.

"Mama, we have a Heatless Day, a Meatless Day, a Sugarless Day," Henny said, grinning. "Why don't they make a Homeworkless Day?"

For Grace the busy days had their moments of emptiness. "If only we knew what happened," she kept saying to Ella.

"Maybe Jules will be able to tell us something," Ella would say. But even as she spoke, she felt panic. Here it was, late in February, and no letter from Jules.

March blew in with a chilly wind, but brought with it a letter from Jules at last.

He had been wounded, Jules wrote, but not seriously. He was in a hospital in France, but would be back with his company in a month.

Jules knew little about what had happened to Bill, except that he had volunteered for night patrol on a dangerous assignment. He had not returned to his unit, and nothing had been heard from him.

It was spring. People tightened their belts and went grimly about their work. Another letter came from Jules in which he said that he was completely recovered and back on active duty. So once again fear for his safety nagged at Ella. Mama noticed the shadows deepening on Ella's face. "Ella, there's nothing like work to help you forget trouble," she pointed out. And Ella resolved to heed Mama's advice. She loved dramatics, so she threw herself wholeheartedly into directing plays at Sunday school. For every important Jewish holiday she had the children present a play. Now she was rehearsing the biblical story of Ruth and Naomi for Shavuos, the Feast of Weeks.

Shavuos, which comes seven weeks after Passover, commemorates a festival that was held in Palestine in ancient times when the Jews were farmers. At this season of the year, they had finished gathering in their crops. Rejoicing in the harvest, they celebrated by making a pilgrimage to Jerusalem. Each one brought to the Temple the first fruits of his crop, wheat or barley, dates or figs, olive oil, grapes and pomegranates. This was to remind them that everything on the earth belongs to the Lord and that man is but the caretaker.

At Shavuos, those who had rich fields were expected to share with the poor and the stranger. The needy were allowed to follow after the gleaners so that they might pick up the fallen grain, or to cut the grain in a corner of the field that was set aside especially for them.

But even more important—Shavuos is the birthday of the Jewish religion. It was at this time that Moses received the Ten Commandments from God on Mount Sinai to give to his people.

One Sunday the children came home from Sunday school, fluttering with excitement. "Mama," Gertie cried, "guess what! You know the play we're rehearsing with Ella? Well—we're going to charge admission and give the money to the Red Cross!"

"That's very good," Mama said. "Whose idea was that?"

"Henny's!" Sarah told her.

"I asked permission from the principal," Henny said proudly, "and he said yes."

"But now that it's all settled," Ella chimed in, "I'm scared to death. Suppose it doesn't turn out well?"

Mama smiled. "It will."

The next three weeks were crowded with preparations for the big event. Ella's guiding hand was in everything. Other teachers did the sewing, but it was Ella who designed the costumes. The scenery was being put together by the older boys, under Ella's watchful eye, and with Ella doing much of the painting. It was Henny who worked out the dances, but it was Ella who offered suggestions. Sometimes she came home in high spirits. Everything was going along fine. Sometimes she despaired of everything. "Mama," she complained, "that girl who's playing Ruth—she's a good actress, and she certainly looks beautiful on the stage, but she'll never be able to sing Ruth's song. I'm going crazy trying to teach her, but it's just no use. She just hasn't got the voice for it."

"Don't take it so to heart," Papa consoled her. "I'm sure no one expects her to be an opera singer. Besides, it's a friendly audience, just the parents and relatives and neighbors. Ten years from now, who'll remember who sang?"

Henny clapped her hands. Her eyes sparkled. "That's it!" she shouted. Rushing over to Ella, she whispered excitedly into her ear. Ella's face lit up.

"What is it? What is it?" the sisters clamored. But neither Ella nor Henny would tell.

Then Shavuos was here. Friends and relatives brought gifts of plants and fruits and shared in the eating of the customary dairy foods that were served for this holiday.

On the Sunday afternoon of the performance, the Hebrew School auditorium was packed. The Healys had been invited to see the play they had heard so much about. They sat in the same row with Papa, Mama, Charlie, Lena, Uncle Hyman, and Mrs. Shiner.

Backstage was bedlam. Ella and Henny rushed about pinning squirming youngsters into their costumes, putting make-up on their faces, giving last minute instructions, and, in between, hissing, "Shush! They'll hear you outside!"

At the very final moment, Ella yanked away from the curtain a small boy who was peeping out and waving to his mama and papa.

The curtain went up. A spotlight revealed a little girl standing at one side of the stage. She began to read:

> "And it came to pass that there was a famine in the land of Judah. And a certain man of Bethlehem went to live in the fields of Moab, he and his wife, and his two sons. And the man was named Elimelich and his wife was named Naomi . . .
>
> Elimelich died. And the two sons took wives of the women of Moab—the name of the one was Orpah and the name of the other Ruth, and they dwelt there about ten years. And the sons died and the three women were left widowed. Naomi wished to return to the land of her fathers, and Ruth and Orpah went with her through the fields to the road that led to Bethlehem . . ."

"Isn't that from the Bible?" Mrs. Healy whispered to Papa.

"Well, it's not exactly like we read it in the synagogue. I suppose they made it simple so the children would understand."

The reader closed her book and disappeared. The stage lights brightened.

"See, Charlie," Mama said softly, "that's Ruth, and that's Orpah, and there is Naomi."

Charlie scoffed. "Nah! That's not Naomi. That's Sarah. She's dressed up like an old lady."

Naomi stretched out her arms and began to speak in a broken voice. "Alas, soon it will be dark. Return you now to your homes."

And Orpah, weeping bitterly, embraced Naomi and departed.

Then Naomi said to Ruth, "Dearest Ruth, go you too as Orpah has done. I am an old woman, but you are still young. Your husband is dead, but here in the land of Moab you have many relatives and friends. You will find happiness with them again."

But no matter how much Naomi urged, Ruth would not leave. Lifting her head, she began to sing. The audience grew still under the spell of the lovely voice, so full and strong, yet so tender.

Papa and Mama exchanged bewildered glances. The voice —they knew it so well! But how could it be? There was the girl on stage singing the role of Ruth. Her mouth moved in song. Her whole body seemed alive with the music. They listened intently. "It *is* Ella singing!" Mama whispered.

"No mistake about it," Papa whispered back.

They marveled how cleverly it was being done. Ruth's lips moved perfectly in time with Ella's backstage singing. Pure and clear were the beautiful words of devotion that have come down through the ages:

> Entreat me not to leave thee
>> And to return from following after thee
> For whither thou goest, I will go
>> And where thou lodgest, I will lodge
> Thy people shall be my people
>> And thy God my God.

> Where thou diest, will I die
>> And there will I be buried.
> The Lord do so to me
> And more also
>> If aught but death part thee and me.

The curtain was lowered, and the applause rang out. Murmurs of admiration swelled from all sides of the auditorium. "Such a wonderful voice!"

Mama and Papa smiled at each other.

Grace leaned over and touched Mama's hand. "You know, I would have sworn that was Ella singing."

Mama's eyes twinkled. "You think so?"

Act Two began almost immediately. Once again the reader stood in a circle of light . . .

"Now it happened that Ruth and Naomi came to Bethlehem at the time of the harvest. There was a man called Boaz, kinsman to Naomi, and he had many large fields. And Ruth joined the poor who followed after the gleaners in the fields of Boaz, for it was known that he was kind and generous . . ."

Bright light flooded the stage, and sighs of delight rippled through the audience, so charming was the picture. The golden fields filled with cut sheaves seemed so real that one could almost smell the fallen gleanings. Slowly the gleaners moved across the stage gathering up the grain. Ruth was among them, and the others gazed at her and whispered about her great beauty.

Boaz appeared. "Who is this maiden?" he asked of his gleaners.

"She is the daughter-in-law of thy kinswoman, Naomi. They have just come from the land of Moab."

"Ah, yes, so I have heard. They have suffered much and are in great need. See that you let many stalks fall in the maiden's path."

Then Boaz addressed himself to Ruth. "I bid you welcome. Come to my fields as often as you like for the grain with which to make your bread. You shall eat with my workers when you are hungry, and if you are thirsty, they will draw water for you to drink."

"Why are you so kind to me?" Ruth asked.

And Boaz replied, "It has been told to me all that you have done for Naomi. Who deserves kindness more than you who have been so loyal and generous to an old woman?"

Soon the harvest gatherers laid aside their scythes and sat down to eat and drink and make merry. "Come, let us dance!" cried one, and in a moment a small group leaped to their feet. Among the dancers were Gertie and Charlotte.

The piano gave forth a rollicking tune, and the gleaners burst into song, clapping their hands in rhythm. Skirts billowing gracefully, heads proudly raised, the little dancers circled about. "Did you ever see a prettier sight!" exclaimed Mrs. Healy.

Caught up in the happy beat of the music, the audience began clapping their hands and stamping their feet. Backstage, Ella and Henny hugged each other. "They like it! They really like it!"

Hopping and skipping for all she was worth, Gertie was leading the line of dancers when suddenly she heard—snap! The safety pin holding her skirt band flew open! She could feel the skirt beginning to slip down the back. Desperately she clung to it with one hand, trying to face front all the time. Already some people in the front row were tittering. Oh, dear, what should she do? She turned her head toward the wings, sending appealing glances for help.

Frantically, Ella beckoned to her. Gertie started to dance sideways, forcing herself to smile. But before she could reach the wings, the droopy skirt was trailing on the floor. The titters

grew into boisterous laughter. Gertie's face puckered up. She ran sobbing off the stage.

Ella caught her. "It's all right, Gertie. They're not laughing at you. They're laughing with you!" Quickly she pinned the unruly skirt back into place. "Go on back!" and she gave her a little push.

Sniffling a little, Gertie skipped back to her place among the dancers. The audience applauded loudly.

"They're clapping for you," Charlotte murmured to Gertie as she danced by.

"Honest?" Gertie asked, and her eyes glowed.

Without further mishap, the play went into Act Three. Boaz, the rich landowner, grew to love Ruth; they were married and lived happily ever after. Thus the play ended. Everyone agreed that it had been a huge success.

That night the family sat around the table eating the traditional *blintzes,* the pancakes filled with sweetened cheese that everyone loved. The talk was of nothing but the play. "Just think," Ella said, "besides all the fun we had, we made one hundred and twenty-five dollars for the Red Cross!"

"Ella, I thought you said the girl who played Ruth couldn't sing a note," Papa remarked, merry crinkles showing around his eyes.

Laughter rolled around the table. "Wasn't it amazing the way it was done?" Sarah said, enthusiastically. "The audience never even guessed."

"It was Henny's idea," Ella put in. "You were really smart, Henny."

"Nope. Not at all," replied Henny. "Actually it was Papa who gave me the idea."

Papa looked puzzled. "Who? Me?"

"Don't you remember, Papa? You said, 'ten years from now, who'll remember who sang?' That's when it came to me like a flash!"

"Well, so I'm the smart one!" Papa exclaimed, looking pleased at everyone.

The History Prize

Sarah had studied hard. Her head felt crammed full of history—dates, names, and places. All year her work in class had won praise from Miss Brady. Even her classmates kept assuring her, "You'll surely win the prize!"

Sarah bore in mind, however, that it wasn't enough to be tops in the daily classwork. She had to get the highest mark in all the tests as well. Or at least, as high as her rival, Dorothy Miller. Up till now, things had gone just fine.

At last the morning came for the most important test of all—the final exam. Everything would depend upon this test. "I'm scared!" Sarah whispered to Dorothy as the class filed into Miss Brady's room.

"I'm not. I know my work!" boasted Dorothy.

She looks as calm as a cucumber, Sarah thought enviously. She could feel her own heart beating with hammer blows. Tensely she kept twisting and untwisting her hands in her lap.

Miss Brady passed out sheets of paper. Presently she was writing the questions on the blackboard. Sarah's eyes followed the squeaking movement of the chalk across the board. Stop worrying! It's going to be all right! she encouraged herself.

As her pen went scratching along the lines of the paper, she forgot her worry. She wrote speedily, hesitating only once when she came to a question about the French and Indian War. She wasn't sure of the answer. She chewed her penholder thoughtfully. Finally she made up her mind. Once more her head bent over the paper before her. She finished answering the last question just as the bell rang. It was all over!

"Wasn't it just awful!" "The hardest test we ever had!" the girls exclaimed to one another. Then they fell to comparing answers. Sarah remained silent. She went home and looked up the French and Indian War, and still she wasn't sure.

Miss Brady never told what your final marks were. You had to wait for graduation day, when you got your report card. Sarah worried, but everyone in school was certain that she'd be the first-prize winner.

At home Sarah talked of nothing else, till Mama finally said, with some concern, "Listen, Sarah, I've told you over and over, you've got to understand that winning is not the most important thing. What is important is that a person should do the very best he can, whether he wins a prize or not. You did that. So even if you don't win, we'll all be just as proud of you."

For the whole year, during sewing periods in school, Sarah and her classmates had worked on their graduation dresses. They were made entirely by hand, and every stitch had to be perfect. Sometimes Sarah felt she was doing as much ripping as sewing, but at long last her dress was completed. It was made of white nainsook, high waisted and full skirted, with little white rosebuds trimming the neck and tiny puffed sleeves. Washed, starched, and ironed by Mama, it really looked beautiful.

The night before the graduation ceremony, Henny put up Sarah's hair in rag curls, and in the morning Sarah again had her cherished curls tumbling down her back.

Wonderful, wonderful graduation day! Sarah's usually pale face was pink with excitement. She would be reciting a poem in assembly today! She'd stand right up in front, on the platform where the principal and all the important people would be sitting! She had rehearsed over and over with Miss Brady. "Say it naturally in your own lovely voice," Miss Brady had told her, "and it'll be fine." And then there was the history prize!

Assembly began quite differently today. In two long lines, the graduates, all dressed in white, marched proudly to their seats.

The principal came forward and welcomed the parents and guests. Then Sarah recited her poem. It went well. She could

tell from the way everyone smiled approvingly at her. Then there was music, singing, and speeches, and more speeches.

Now! Now the prizes were to be given out! Sarah felt a tingle running up and down her spine. On the platform, the principal was announcing the names of the various winners. Arithmetic...geography... Sarah stretched forward, listening with all her might. Would they never get to history? History ... The principal held up a book. *"The Life of George Washington,* won by—" Sarah half-rose in her seat—"Dorothy Miller!"

There must be some mistake, Sarah thought confusedly. It can't be! It can't be! But there was Dorothy walking with head high down the center aisle toward the platform. The blood pounded at Sarah's temples. The pain inside her was unbearable. She could feel the eyes of all her classmates upon her. No one must see how terrible she felt. She forced herself to smile.

Afterwards she congratulated Dorothy and went about getting her autograph album signed.

"Gee, that was a surprise!" "I was sure you'd be the winner, Sarah!" "I'm awfully sorry!" It was hard to have to listen to the girls saying these things. How she longed to get away from everyone! As soon as she could, she edged toward the door and out into the hallway.

Close by the stairs she bumped into Miss Brady. "Good luck, Sarah." Miss Brady took hold of Sarah's hand. She said nothing more, but her eyes studied the girl's face. Sarah struggled hard to keep from crying. "Good-by," she mumbled, pulling her hand away and rushing down the stairs. Tears blinded her eyes. It wasn't fair! She had worked so hard! She deserved the prize. Everyone said so! Everyone!

At home no one mentioned the prize. Sarah could feel everyone trying to be extra kind, telling her how well she had recited and how nice she had looked. But for Sarah, the long-looked-forward-to day was now empty of magic. She counted the minutes till bedtime when she could be by herself.

Next morning a parcel was delivered to Mama's house, and they all gathered around to examine it. "It's for you, Sarah," Charlotte said. "It must be a graduation present. Quick, Sarah, open it up and let's see!"

"Who sent it?" asked Gertie.

Ella turned the surprise package over. "It doesn't say anywhere. Sarah, open it up!"

Sarah began fumbling with the knot. "Oh, you slowpoke!" Henny cried. Snatching up a kitchen knife, she snipped the cord and hastily tore away the wrapping.

There was lots and lots of straw and paper first, then underneath, carefully folded in tissue paper, lay a handsome black leather-bound book with gleaming gilt-edged pages. "Why, it's a dictionary!" cried Sarah. "Did you ever see anything so beautiful?"

It was indeed the biggest, the handsomest dictionary they had ever seen. There were pages and pages of bright colored pictures—costumes of ancient times, precious stones, flowers, flags of the world, strange animals, and many, many other fascinating things. Sarah perked up. "This will be a lot of help when I get to high school," she said. "I wonder who sent it?"

As her fingers caressed the soft leather binding, a little card fell out. Sarah opened it and immediately recognized the bold handwriting:

> To Sarah,
>   For the joy and pleasure she gave to her teacher
> by her outstanding work in history.
>   Lillian Brady
> P.S. See page 1176 for the correct answer on the
> French and Indian War.

Sarah hugged the book to her. "Oh!" she gasped, and tears sprang to her eyes. Only this time they were tears of joy.

Homecoming

Sarah sat on the bed watching her sister coil her long, dark hair into a neat bun. "That looks nice, Ella," she said. She gave herself a little hug. "Aren't you glad it's such a lovely day?"

"Uh-huh. Perfect for a parade!" Ella replied happily, as she slipped her red woolen dress over her head. Her fingers trembled so much that she had trouble sliding the gold buttons into the buttonholes. It had been so long, so very, very long! Now at last it was over—all the worrying, the longing, the waiting!

She glanced up at the bold, black letters on the newspaper headline pasted across her mirror. "Germany Surrenders!"

She thought about that morning four months ago—November 11, 1918. She would never forget it!

Up and down the city streets the newsboys had raced. "Extra! Extra! Read all about it! Victory for the Allies! Armistice signed!" People had rushed out to get papers. Again she heard the wild shouting, the whistles blowing, and the ringing of the bells. Once more she could see the joyous dancing in the streets, strangers embracing one another. "We've won!" President Wilson had announced, "The war thus comes to an end!"

"For heaven's sake, Ella!" Henny's impatient voice startled Ella out of her thoughts. "The parade'll be over by the time we get there!"

"Ella has to look her best," Mama said, with an indulgent smile. "Today is more than extra special for her."

"Yes, but it's the Victory Parade!" Henny insisted. "There'll be a mob. If we don't get there early, we'll never find a place to stand."

Charlie was equally impatient. "When are we going to the parade?" He looked so adorable in his new sailor suit that Ella had to bend down and give him a hug. "I've got something for you," she said. She took out a small flag from her closet and began to unfurl it.

"No! No! Let me do it!" shouted Charlie, stretching out eager hands. "I wanna open it myself!"

Flag on his shoulder, he stamped around the room, shouting, "Left, right, left, right!"

As the family came downstairs, they found themselves whispering when they passed the Healy door. If only they could be welcoming Bill home today as well as Jules! Ella felt sad when she thought of unhappy Grace.

"Why do we have to go so far downtown?" Charlotte asked, when they were on the train. "Isn't the parade going all the way up on Fifth Avenue?"

"If we go down to Twenty-third Street, we'll see the soldiers go through the Victory Arch," Papa said. "It's not going to stand there forever, you know. It'll be pulled down as soon as all the boys are home."

"Then why did they bother to put it up in the first place?" inquired Gertie.

"It's a custom," Ella explained, "welcoming home a victorious army with a victory arch."

It was still too early for the parade when they reached their destination, but already thousands of people were crowding the curbs. His flag borne proudly aloft, Charlie held tightly to Papa's hand.

The streets wore a holiday air. Banners floated from office buildings and brownstone houses, with red, white, and blue decorations everywhere. And the Victory Arch! Right in the middle of the Square it soared, dazzlingly white in the sun, a magnificently ornamented central arch supported by smaller arches on either side. On top was a statue, colossal in size, of a large chariot drawn by six spirited horses and bearing a triumphant figure carrying a flag. On the smaller arches were placed four figures, representing Peace, Justice, Power, and Wisdom. Elaborately carved pillars lined the roadway leading to the entrance.

"Look, Charlie," Papa pointed upward, "how'd you like to take a ride in the sky?" Charlie stared heavenward at two giant balloons that floated from the top of the central arch.

They waited and waited. "When are they going to start the parade?" Charlie kept asking.

"I'm getting tired standing," Gertie complained.

Mama spread a newspaper on the curbstone, and grownups good-naturedly moved aside to let the youngsters sit down. Suddenly, from a distance, they could hear "Boom, boom, boom!" and the sound of stirring music. "Here they come!" "Look at them!" The crowd surged forward, pressing against the lines of policemen.

Up the avenue they came, twenty thousand strong, with flags flying and bands playing. In the lead rode their general, mounted on a white horse. The people broke into wild cheers and waved frantically.

As the troops passed in review, there were many who showed the scars of battle; some limped and some had their arms in slings. But they stepped forward beneath the forest of

flags with a pride that thrilled everyone. It was as if they were saying, "We saw it through!"

All the while, Ella was searching for Jules. He must see her to know how proud she was of him. Her eyes lit on a face that seemed familiar; it was lean and tanned a ruddy brown. Was it really Jules? My, how manly he looked! The family leaped about, yelling excitedly, "Jules! Jules!"

But Jules, every inch the soldier, marched stiffly by without once turning his head or missing a step. In another moment, he and his comrades were passing through the Victory Arch.

At the end of the procession, a large flag covered with gold stars came into view, and the onlookers grew still in memory of those who had given their lives for their country. Papa shook his head sadly. "There must be a star for Bill," he said.

"Carry me upstairs, Papa," Charlie implored as they approached the stoop. "I'm tired."

"We're all tired," said Papa, giving Charlie's nose a little tweak. "So why don't you carry me upstairs?"

Charlie giggled and yawned at the same time as Papa lifted him in his arms, and the weary family plodded into the hallway.

The Healys' doors were wide open. Something unusual was going on. As they passed, they could hear shrill and excited talking and what sounded like weeping. What was the matter? The family exchanged startled glances. "Something terrible must have happened!" Mama cried out in alarm. She rushed into the Healy parlor, everyone at her heels.

Mama stopped short, bewildered at the strange sight before her. Grace was on the couch, hands covering her face, sobbing convulsively. Mrs. Healy was standing beside her, exclaiming over and over, "Glory be! Glory be!" Mr. Healy, his face as red as a beet, was hopping around the table and shouting.

Catching sight of the family, Mrs. Healy waved a piece of yellow paper at them. "It's wonderful, wonderful!"

Grace lifted her head. Her face was tear-stained but happy. "It's a telegram from Bill! He's alive! He was in a German prison camp all the time!"

Later, when the family was gathered around the supper table, Papa said, "Now that Ella's young man is back, I guess I'll have to give up smoking."

Mama glanced at him skeptically. "What do you mean?"

"Well, after all," Papa's eyes twinkled, "I have to start saving every extra penny for her dowry."

"Papa!" protested Ella, her face flaming.

"Yes," Henny added, "from now on, all we'll hear around here is Jules, Jules, Jules!"

"You know what I think, Henny," Sarah teased, "you're just jealous because you don't have a boy friend of your own."

"When I grow up, I'm going to be a soldier and march in parades," Charlie announced.

Gertie patted his head fondly. "I thought you wanted to be a fireman."

Charlie cocked his head and thought a moment. "Well, maybe I'll be a cowboy instead," he decided.

"Can you imagine the fascinating stories Bill will be telling, being in a prison camp and everything?" Charlotte exclaimed.

"What a miracle!" Mama said fervently. She put her hand to her cheek. "I still can't believe it."

"Yes, Mama." Papa nodded his head. He lit his pipe and looked around at his family. "God has been good to us. We have managed to live through all this terrible time, and now the world is at peace."